All
We
Know
of
Love

Broadway Books
New York

All
We
Know
of
Love

*

KATIE
SCHNEIDER

BROADWAY

Broadway Books titles may be purchased for business or promotional use or for special sales. For information, please write to: Special Markets Department, Random House, Inc., 1540 Broadway, New York, NY 10036.

BROADWAY BOOKS and its logo, a letter B bisected on the diagonal, are trademarks of Broadway Books, a division of Random House, Inc.

Visit our website at www.broadwaybooks.com

Library of Congress Cataloging-in-Publication Data
Schneider, Katie, 1966–
All we know of love / Katie Schneider.—1st ed.
p.   cm.
1. Americans—Travel—Italy—Fiction.
2. Women artists—Italy—Fiction.
3. Young women—Italy—Fiction.   I. Title.
PS3569.C47929 A79 2000
813'.54—dc21   99-088592

FIRST EDITION

Designed by Claire Naylon Vaccaro

ISBN 0-7679-0408-7

00 01 02 03 04 10 9 8 7 6 5 4 3 2 1

In
Memory
of
Rojer
McRea

All
We
Know
of
Love

My grandfather spent his life mending fences. So much of his life that it seemed like a religion. *Thou shalt not let thy barbed wire sag.* On our farm, Frank single-handedly built a straight line of barbed wire that stretched for acres. He attacked repetitive work like prayer; for him, it was a kind of Zen meditation, a fingering of rosary beads. Dig holes, drive posts, splice wire. Dig holes, drive posts, splice wire.

Frank's sharp and shining metal fences were not about keeping anyone out or, for that matter, keeping anything in. They marked his territory, squarely for all to see. Frank knew every inch of ground on his property—he'd walked and worked and fenced it all, from the time he was a boy shooting groundhogs with his .22 right up to the day he became housebound with bone cancer. He might've said it was his destiny, that farmland, those dry pine woods that came to him through *his* grandfather. The straighter the fence, the clearer the connection to the past, the better the possibility for the future.

That is one of the things I always understood about my grandfather, his curious attachment to fences, and I guess I have always had it too. Otherwise, I wouldn't be here in the high desert of eastern Washington, dressed in heavy jeans and steel-toed boots on a ninety-degree day, working on the line. I wouldn't be on the farm at all, much less out in the front pasture. Frank died six years ago, so there is no one here to make me do it. There is no one back at the house to ask me how it went.

The ground underneath my feet bakes in the yellow gold sun. I wear a baseball hat to keep the light out of my eyes, leather gloves to keep the barbed wire from catching my skin. Sweat trickles down my back, collects in the brim of my hat. Dust, from the field and the gravel on the county road, sticks to the damp hairs on my forearms. The fence line, standing straight and proud, shimmers in waves of heat that steal the horizon. It hurts my eyes to look.

The earth pulses with the lazy singsong saw of crickets. In this part of the country, where the hills roll golden gray into one another for miles at a time, the sky is unbelievably big. There are no buildings to blot it out, to get in the way of the clouds that gather and part on the whim of a powerful wind. From this spot, I can see the curve of the world.

I approach my task methodically. Where the fence has slackened under seasons of hard frost and heavy snows, quick thaws and rain, I tighten new stretches of wire around the metal posts. I use a special tool, made just for fencing, a hammer and pliers and wire cutters all in one. It is solid, unambiguous, and fits in the palm of my leather-bound hand. There is a pleasure in that, uncomplicated and real.

My name is Joanna, after John the Evangelist. I am finally home and it has been a long time since I've worked like this, wrestling with spools of wire. I admit that it is no coincidence that I chose to tackle this job first. It could've easily been the roof on the house, which has sprung a leak into the living room, or the linoleum that's pulling free in the bathroom. But I chose the fence line because I want to bake. I want to sweat. Effort will purify me.

✴

In the early part of this century, the Virgin Mary appeared to three children in Fátima, Portugal. The pasture where they saw her is now a plaza in which tourists congregate and nuns pass back and forth on their knees in supplication. A small chapel stands over the actual site of the apparition, the bush that Mary touched with the tips of her toes.

Iron candle racks stand on one side of that plaza. People bring tapers the size of their prayers, some large, some small, some the actual shape of their affliction.

Shopkeepers sell candles in the village, pieces of wax shaped like arms and legs, or the heads of babies, along with post-cards and rosaries and T-shirts, shot glasses and sunglasses adorned with the image of the Madonna.

At night, the plaza is quiet. For all the tour buses and motels, Fátima remains a rural place. Civilization is just a veneer, a patina that fades with the dusk. But once all is dark and still, an attentive soul hears what has been missed during the day, among the crush of people and the fervent prayers—the whisper of the divine, the voice of God, carried on the flames of two hundred burning candles.

I stand at my kitchen sink in eastern Washington, washing my hands after a day out on the line. The view is unspectacular: a bit of the front pasture, a corner of the barn, the straight line of the fence, the blur of trees that marks the creek. A strange thought occurs to me: I imagine a sea of people out there, a priest inside here by my side. To help the faithful on crutches and in wheelchairs, the field is paved with concrete. Pilgrims carry plaster images, sold in town. They pray the rosary and ask for me, or for a drink of water from my tap. At night, volunteers fill glass bottles with water from our well.

I smile at the idea of all this happening here. But if I tell about what I have seen in this kitchen, it could.

W hen I was five, my mother Susie—who had been raising me in a trailer park on the outskirts of Spokane—got drunk and drove her Dodge Dart into a tree. From there, the car ricocheted into the river, where she drowned. It all happened quickly, the accident and the retrieval of her body. The rescue crew, who thought she might still be alive, pulled her out of the crumpled wreck exactly one hour before the baby-sitter managed to get me to bed.

So my grandfather was the one who raised me. Frank spanked me when I wandered out of the house and into the cow pasture. He held me on his lap and rubbed my feet when they were cold. He taught me how to read. And we lived a kind of normal life until I turned eighteen.

Frank was diagnosed with cancer the summer before I was due to go to college. Despite his illness, he urged me to stick to our plans. He even took me to the bank, had me sign papers to open a new account, deposited the tuition, plus a living allowance, directly into it. "They tell me I have a long time left," he said. They did tell him that, but I also saw the expressions on their faces when they talked to him, the patronizing way they laughed at his jokes. For doctors in a hospital, chatting with a seventy-year-old man with tubes in his arms and a cut in his scrotum where his testicles used to be, three years might have seemed like a long time. But when they were talking about the only father I had ever known, it didn't seem that way to me.

I may have been young, but I wasn't stupid.

※

At eight in the morning, Chuck Riley pulls into my driveway. He is driving a tow truck with his name painted on the side. Last I heard, Chuck had bought the garage over on Main. He'd also married Rene, the girl he had dated in high school. I'm not sure how he knows I'm here, but Bright River is like that, a small town where good news circulates quickly and bad news travels even faster. And secrets, in order to be kept, have to be buried so deeply that they may rot before they're uncovered.

It is comforting to see him, a heavyset man in a truck with stubble on his cheeks and a soiled baseball cap on his head. If it would not have scandalized him, I might've walked straight up to the truck, reached my arm around his neck and kissed him full on the lips. As it is, I settle for leaning on the cab, and tap once on the back of his hand with my index finger.

Chuck grins. "Hey," he says, as if I had seen him yesterday, not six years ago at the occasion of Frank's funeral. He has gained weight since high school. I halfway wonder whether, under that cap, he is bald.

"Hey yourself."

"I bring messages from the outside world."

Chuck's voice sounds green to me, as if the water in it reaches into the dry parts of my soul, soaking them with life. I take a deep breath and my chest expands. The air smells sweet. "I'd offer you coffee, but I haven't got any."

"That brings me directly to point number one. Rene has packed two bags of groceries for you. There is fried chicken in one of the bags and it needs to go into the refrigerator."

Before I can so much as nod, Chuck moves on. "Second, Mrs. Stanley at the library wants you to call her."

I do not care about Mrs. Stanley. I do not care about much of anything, except for the fact that Chuck still exists, that the farm and the pastures have survived just fine, that there is a corner of the universe that seems to belong to me.

"She says to tell you that it has something to do with Hazel Potts."

The name seems vaguely familiar, like the smell of a flower that used to grow in someone else's backyard. But I am more preoccupied with the beauty of my own trees, a line of poplars my great-grandfather planted as a break against the fierce wind. They stand straight and silver-green against a cloudless sky.

"Third, I have come to look at the truck to make sure it runs because if it doesn't, then you are stuck and you will starve to death."

The truck is Frank's truck, a 1954 International, gunmetal gray. It has no seats, only pine boards covered with sofa cushions. There is still half a roll of his peppermint Lifesavers in the glove compartment.

"It worked yesterday."

"Doesn't mean it'll work tomorrow. Get me the key?"

"Sure."

He pauses. "Have you talked to Jack yet?"

He means Jack Pearce, his best friend, my best friend from a long time ago. He lives in Seattle now, climbs Mount Rainier for a living and sells equipment to people who want to follow him. Chuck and Rene have been trying to fix us up since we were twelve years old.

"Jesus. I just got here day before yesterday."

"You didn't tell him you were coming home, did you?"

I walk toward the back to get the groceries. That way, he can't see the shaking of my hands. "What makes you think that?"

"The fact that he tried to call your number in New York and then called us when it was disconnected."

"Well."

I set one bag by a tire, hold the other in my arms. Chuck looks at me. I stare back. I know him well enough to be sure that he doesn't have the patience I do.

Finally, Chuck shrugs. "You're not going to tell me what happened, are you?"

"If it makes you feel any better, I'm not telling anybody else either." I head back up on the porch with the bag full of food. "I'll make you some coffee, though, if Rene put any in here."

"Of course she did." And like a good parent, he can't help himself from finishing with one last protective question. "Are you sure you're going to be okay here by your-self?"

He knows I am without family. He knows, too, that my economic health is always in question. I am an artist, both by profession and by temperament. I am attracted to color and shape, often to the exclusion of practical matters. For Chuck, the artwork I create is akin to collecting cats, the hobby of the perpetually lonely, the spinsters and hermits of the world. He cares for me, but wonders whether I am slightly strange.

I can't say that I blame him.

※

Two and a half years after high school gradua-tion, after everyone my age had escaped from our small town, I woke Frank at midnight so he could take his pills. We had a routine, a series of moves perfected by practice and necessity. I pulled the heavy blankets off his body, then held out a hand. He would grip it tightly, then use the lever-age to maneuver himself around, legs off the edge of the bed, his head running crossways. Then I would help him sit up. He had to do as much by himself as he could, otherwise I might have hurt him. Once he was in position, I wrapped a quilt around his skeletal feet. Then I knelt there, on the floor, and handed him pills, one by one.

Some days, Frank offered to go into a nursing home. He thought he meant it. I knew he didn't. When the pain became too much for him to fall asleep, I read descriptions from the Territorial Seed catalog, as if we would have another garden, as if he would be alive another season. No one in a managed-care environment would have listed the merits of pole beans, conjured up the illusion of pink and purple sweet peas. Frank had not left me in an orphanage. I refused to put him in a home.

Still, one night in particular, he swallowed with such deliberation that it made me scared for him, scared for me. What would I do when his throat closed down completely, when even the slick gelatin capsules lodged there to choke him? It was then that it struck me, how tired I was, tired of getting up at midnight and again at six, tired of counting out meds into plastic pill boxes with seven compartments, one for every day of the week. I was tired of buying eggs that Frank was supposed to eat, but couldn't get down. I was tired of running into Mrs. Sherman from down the road, who wanted a blow-by-blow account of every doctor's visit, each blood transfusion. I was tired of the town's sympathy, I was tired of the town's disdain, the men down at the diner who had never quite forgiven my mother for flashing her bare breasts at the drive-in in Spokane, showing it all, but not to them.

Frank rarely spoke at night, except that particular night he did, as if he sensed how much I needed to hear his voice, to hear someone's voice, to pull me back from the black edge of exhaustion. "Thank you," he whispered, with the terrible graciousness of a man who was dying. "Thank you for doing this for me."

It was finally quiet enough, I suppose, to admit that I was terrified. I leaned back on my heels. I looked at him. Tears filled my eyes. "What am I going to do?"

He smiled then, a genuine smile, one of the last ones I ever saw, saved and preserved in just that glimmer of light, framed in the rumple of bedclothes. My grandfather knew, in his head, what he was going to say, long before he could form the words.

"How the hell am I supposed to know?"

The abruptness of his humor made me laugh.

✳

Later that night, the Virgin Mary appeared to me in the kitchen. First came the smell, an overpowering scent of lilacs and the hint of yellow linden blossoms. Then color exploded, a lush jungle green as if the world had just been created and every magical place from my childhood imagination sprang forth in front of me, taking over the gray of the house. Waxed leaves wrapped around the rafters, dripping fertile tropical humidity over the linoleum floor.

And then I heard the voice, which sounded like my own. "Do not be afraid" is what I heard. Angels had said it to her once upon a time, but it wasn't the right phrase for me, because I wasn't scared as much as curiously and completely full, as if everything I had ever wanted had simply been granted to me. Mary was surrounded by white light, a light that consumed my body until there was no more of me left in darkness. I remember silence and the far-off buzzing of a single fly.

Then I woke up to an empty house with a night-light on in the hallway, consumed by the physical sensation of being alone and hollow and abandoned, left wanting and needing and gasping for more.

❋

We watched Frank, the hospice nurses and I, watched when he stopped eating, stood by when he stopped drinking water, when he closed his lips even to slivers of ice. A neighbor from our church read the Bible out loud, her voice droning over the sound of his labored breathing and the rattle of the fan I kept on to carry away the sour sick smell of his decaying breath.

I was doing the laundry the day he died, sitting on a folding chair in front of the dryer, watching sheets tumble behind a glass door. I was tired and afraid and couldn't help but be mesmerized by the simple rhythm of yellow cotton tossed up and down. I could not keep constant watch against death.

And that was when Frank drifted away, while I was in the basement. For the first time in weeks, no one was violating his privacy, no one listening for labored breathing over the baby monitor in the living room. When I went back upstairs to check on him, Frank was simply gone, his body wasted, dry and empty. I backed out of the room, couldn't stay there any longer, couldn't feel any relief at all.

I fled out into the yard, through the garage, down by the rosebushes. They were in full pink bloom, threatening to take over the adjacent flower beds. I hadn't thought to cut them back that year. It was strange, each leaf and petal and thorn had been thrown into stark relief. Frank's death had changed everything. And it had changed nothing at all.

I found myself standing in the garden, staring at the bushy green tops of the potatoes. I could've fallen to my knees right then, dug down into the soft dirt with my bare hands. Frank preferred to go after them that way. Shovels cut into the meat of the tuber, ruining them. But Frank was dead, in the house, in a bed overlooking the garden. I caught sight of his white-sheeted feet through the window.

The men from the funeral home were efficient, quiet, and tactful. So were the men from the hospital-supply store who came to extract the special bed where Frank had died. It had left marks in the carpet from its weight. A hospice nurse came to the door—I had forgotten to call to let her know we wouldn't be needing her. She began to cry, there on the porch, grieving with an ease I envied.

I know I should've made some move to comfort her, I should've had it in me to be generous. But when it came to her tears, I stood, stone-faced and closed-fisted, wondering how long it might be before I could start to pack. Because I already knew by then that I was going to Italy, that I was going to use the money Frank had put aside for my college to go to Europe and become a painter. The Virgin Mary had told me so.

TWO

One of the things I couldn't understand was why, in my vision, Mary wasn't dressed in blue and white, why her features were so narrow, the cast of her skin so green. She wore a black cloak with a gold star on the shoulder, her eyes were almond shaped in the style of the Byzantines, her fingers curved and thin, like the tines of a pitchfork. It didn't make sense—she didn't look like the Virgin on the altar of Saint Aloysius back in Spokane or the Madonna in any of my Christmas stories. And I didn't understand until I got off the plane in Milan, traveled by train across to Venice, down into Bologna, until I made it all the way to Florence, walked into the Uffizi Gallery and came face-to-face with a painting by Giotto in the first room at the top of the stairs. And there she was.

The sight of her knocked me to the ground, the acrid smell of fire filling my nostrils. It was as if I had forgotten how to stand on my own, how to use the muscle groups that kept me upright. A shade was drawn, blocking out normal light and normal sound. Then out of the darkness came a single voice, aimless and quiet, as if a woman were humming under her breath to a child. But what a child it must have been to inspire the harmonies I heard, each note the creation of a planet, each pause the blackness of space in between.

The very sweet British woman who revived me said, quite politely, that I had fainted. A guard helped me to a nearby chair, then went off to fetch a glass of water. The woman asked me whether I had been ill, but then I looked again at that work of art, the almost-smile on the Virgin Mary's face, the calm eyes of the baby Jesus, and I knew it had been the woman of my vision. She had reached into my chest with those thin fingers and soothed my grieving heart.

The angels in the painting had rainbow-colored wings, lines of soft pink and cream and green. They knelt at the Madonna's feet and stood beside her throne, staring in adoration. I wanted to bring her gifts the way they did, flowers and gold and myrrh. I wanted her to take me in, to fold me into the painting where I would always be able to hear that music, where I would have a place to be and a task to do, one of many in the choir.

I took it as a sign I should stay, a somewhat risky move since my vision had been long on emotion, but short on actual detail. I had the money from my college fund, but nowhere to go; some idea of what I wanted, but not how to go about getting it. My tourist guidebook, written by students from Harvard, did not include a section on miracles.

It took a little more than a week to find a room I could afford in the house of a widow named Lena Cabrini. The ceiling in my room was low and the bed narrow, but the arthritic signora needed help with errands and offered a lower rent if I would do her domestic chores. Something about taking care of an aging woman, after I'd just finished taking care of a dying man, made sense to me. I took a deep breath and hung my clothes in the wardrobe, crossed myself before throwing open the window shutters to take in the view of the street.

I struck Florence with a kind of grim determination, walking not out of pleasure but compulsion, a deep need to keep moving before the gears rusted in place. In those first few weeks, nothing was familiar, nothing smelled like woods or looked like fields or felt like the autumn I knew. I remember stone walls and yellow plaster finishes and bright red flowers in window boxes, a crush of people at a stoplight, the diesel roar of orange buses. Those colors melted in my mind into slick chrome surfaces, block after block of coffee bars and glistening glass bottles of liquor behind them, the sound of steam forced through milk, the thump of metal on rubber as espresso grounds were unceremoniously dumped into the trash.

Unable to stop, unwilling to think, I made my way on narrow sidewalks from the signora's house down to the river where men fished from concrete embankments, up to the church of San Miniato, where, according to the myth, the martyr himself ran to be buried, carrying his own severed head. I followed the outlines of the ancient Roman walls past outdoor cafés where wealthy women sat wearing sunglasses and sipping blood red Campari. Looking for Dante's house in the very center of the city, I discovered streets so tiny they didn't have names, so narrow I could stand in the middle of them and reach the buildings on either side with the tips of my outstretched hands.

Foreign words washed over me like water. I couldn't talk and couldn't have understood the Italian even if I'd wanted to. Like a ghost, I haunted strangers' lives, staring at them in a way I've never looked at people before or since. To this day, I can recall individuals I never met moving in slow motion through the business of their day, distorted by time and slightly out of focus: the teenage sons of a butcher taking off blood-smeared white coats, a guard outside a bank holding an Uzi and blowing round gum bubbles, pink and fleeting and strangely adolescent. At dusk, couples kissed in doorways, men's hands groped under the short skirts women wore. Once I passed a man forming a triangle with the wall, forehead against the brick, feet splayed back from it, vomiting on the sidewalk.

I expected divine help to make sense of it all. I

expected a sign that would be impossible to ignore. It was, after all, because of the mother of Christ that I was in Italy in the first place. So, reverting back to a childhood habit, I knelt down at the side of my bed and said my prayers before going to sleep. I went back to the Uffizi, stood in line day after day with the tourists. I pleaded with Mary in my head, staring at the painting, but it never came alive again, was never anything but flat paint and make-believe angels. I prayed to Frank, begged him to show me that he was just around the corner, closer than I thought. I set up tests for him, tests he consistently failed when he didn't make the phone ring, when it didn't start to rain. I wanted to communicate with the dead. They didn't seem to be listening.

I dreamed of Frank instead, nighttime journeys I didn't always remember in the morning, didn't want to remember because the closer I held him to me, the more it hurt when I had to open my eyes, to admit I had left the farm, to admit that he had left me. My mother danced at the edges of those dreams, never quite in the picture. She peeked out over Frank's shoulder, then ducked behind the barn to come out on the other side, to run over to the rosebushes, to pluck the petals off and throw them in the air.

I would wake up to Lena tap, tap, tapping on my door with one knuckle. She brought me coffee in bed in the mornings, left it on my night table about the time she thought I should be getting up. She stood in my doorway, asking permission to enter, which I always granted, since she was doing me a favor, a wonderful favor, as if I were a cherished relative instead of just a boarder. In those instants, I forgot what I had been dreaming.

Then Lena left me with my coffee and I remembered.

✳

Crossing the wide expanse of the Piazza della Repubblica on my way to the river, the September sun was full of promise, as if the days were growing longer instead of shorter, as if winter were a lifetime away. The light skittered across the glossy black hair of the men selling postcards, over the matte gray backs of the pigeons, coming to rest on the white marble copy of David in front of the city hall. It transformed the hills on the outskirts of the city to a smoke blue-gray.

I heard the music first, then saw a knot of people gathered on the side street where automobile traffic had long since been banned. The crowd stood between two shop fronts, a store that sold expensive shoes and a bar with trays of pastries in the window. The music came from a single cello, low tones the frequency of human conversation, languid notes that matched the rhythm of my heartbeat. I squinted into the brilliance of gold and blue air, moved closer to the musician, waded into the crowd.

The man may have been older than me, but not by much. Dressed in loose tweed pants, a white dress shirt, and worn leather shoes, he held the bow in his right hand, lightly, with two or three fingers, and moved his whole body, as if it weren't his fingers doing the work, but the whole strength of his torso. He didn't bother to look at the sheet music, clipped to a stand with a clothespin. Rather, his eyes were closed, as if the music already existed inside him and all he had to do was let it out.

The sound enveloped me, wrapped itself around and seeped in through my skin, down into my heart, my liver, my bones. Frank had never listened to such music, but I could not help but think that, miles and cultures away, the notes had something to do with him. I could see him in Hungarian gypsies and Viennese waltzes, in ballrooms and drawing rooms and peasant fields, the places where this music came from, the sky where it was headed.

There, in the loose knot of quiet admirers, I felt my face tighten against the depth of feeling the music evoked. The melody swelled, then dropped to pianissimo, a whisper that threatened to disappear under the sound of the foot traffic and tourist chatter. Like a single-celled organism, the crowd took a half step forward. The musician drew us in, making sure we were really listening, attentive to the end. Discord resolved into harmony, melodies coming together at the very last.

The musician held his bow up. He plucked the last three notes with his long white fingers. They fell like round pebbles into a pond and whispered as they sank.

When he was finished, the man looked up, smiled briefly in acknowledgment of our applause. Some in the crowd drifted away. Others dug in their pockets for coins, tossed them casually into his velvet-lined case. But I just stood there.

The cellist's eyes fell on me. When they did, I faltered and looked away—my face was sore from the effort of not crying, of not turning to the people immediately next to me and blurting out everything I was feeling. I glanced up at blue sky and wished to be home, where I understood what my response to the world should be. I didn't want this stranger to know what his music had done. But when I glanced back, throwing a thousand-lire note in the case, I saw that he already did.

✳

That night, I asked the widow if I could join her for a glass of sweet wine. We sat in the kitchen, both of us in bathrobes and slippers, Lena with her swollen feet up on an extra chair. Her hair was a kinky mouse brown, thinning and shot through with gray. She breathed heavily, through her nose, as if her sinuses were collapsing under the weight of her arthritis and too many years of cream-filled sauce.

We sat surrounded by pantry shelves, packed from floor to ceiling with olive oil and white beans, pasta in red and white boxes, canned tomatoes of all kinds. Her refrigerator was the size of an American microwave. That was one of my jobs, every day, to stop at the tiny markets that specialized in certain goods: the *macelleria* to pick up red meat, the *latteria* to get milk and eggs, the *fruttivendolo* to buy salad greens. The signora believed in fresh food, not the newly evolving American-style supermarket where everything was measured and weighed by someone else, mass-produced in factories and wrapped in plastic.

Because she had a hard time grasping lids with her knotted joints, Lena gave me the tin of biscotti to open. We dipped the hard almond cookies in the wine to soften them, to make them even sweeter.

"Tell me about America," she said.

I tried to answer her, I really did, but it was difficult, with my limited Italian, to convey much of anything at all. There seemed to be no frame of reference for what I wanted to say, not in Florence where the bricks on some streets dated back to the Romans and the buildings in the city center had been standing longer than the written history of my entire country. I thought of the commercial strip in Spokane, fast-food franchises and used-car dealerships. I imagined the miles of deserted highway stretching through my town, the sage-like smell of santolina and the weathered face of volcanic basalt.

Dry, I remember saying, and big. I mentioned driving and hours of open highway. Mountains, I said, and rivers. But even then, I knew she couldn't understand, because *river* in English didn't mean *river* in Italian, even if the word was the same. The cultivated Arno, which flowed through country settled for centuries, wasn't the Columbia, cutting through acre upon acre of bare raw soil and scabland. The sky wasn't even the same. I didn't know the word for sage-brush and eventually appealed to the movies, John Wayne and the O.K. Corral.

"I don't think I would like it much," the signora said, with a wrinkling of her nose, as if she'd smelled rotten cheese.

"I'm sorry?"

"America would not be good for me."

"Why?"

"No history, no architecture, no art."

"I don't know if you can say that." Although I knew what she meant. There was history, it was just different—full of dirt rather than emperors, cattle rather than the papal court.

"Here you walk across the piazza and imagine you are following the exact footsteps of Lorenzo de' Medici."

"In America," I said, "you can go to the top of the mountain and feel like you're at the edge of the world."

"You have too much space."

"We call it wilderness."

"It must be lonely."

"There are possibilities," I said, meaning the possibilities inherent in stepping off a road and being confronted with nothing but sweeping terrain.

I tried to tell Lena about a childhood trip I had taken with Frank. At a scenic overlook on Mount Rainier, he had lifted me on top of a waist-high stone wall. The mountain dropped away precipitously, a thousand feet into a hazy valley. He held me there, securely, and acted as if he had ordered the view just for me.

Lena didn't understand a word I said. Instinctively, I dragged out my sketchbook and my set of graphite pencils. While we talked, I drew the outline of the wall. By the time I filled in the contours of the valley, the elderly woman began to nod. She told me a story of her father and a trip to the Dolomites. We both ended up with tears in our eyes.

After the signora went to bed, I rinsed the wineglasses, tucked the tin of cookies back on the shelf. I sat back down at the square kitchen table and stared at my sketch. It was out of proportion, haphazardly done. But that didn't matter. It was the first drawing I had managed to complete since Frank died.

I remembered the way it had been windy there, by the side of the road, and that Frank had wrapped me in his jacket. There had been an apple in one pocket and it had fallen onto the ground.

I turned my book to a fresh sheet of paper. I tried to sketch more from memory, the view of the valley, the jagged surfaces of surrounding cliffs, but none of it came easily. At one time, I might have been able to do a better job, but not after the months I'd spent watching Frank wither away. Since his illness, my standards of beauty had irrevocably changed. That night in Lena's kitchen, I realized the extent to which my technical skills had not kept up. After an hour, I gave up working with full sheets of paper and focused on single elements; the profile of a man, a hand holding an apple, a single tree.

By the time the garbage men drove by, yelling at each other and throwing glass in the back of their truck, I had gotten out a second book, taken the biscotti down off the shelf, and switched from water back to wine. And by then, I was no longer working on an elegy to Frank, but trying to remember the gaze of the cellist in the square. That memory was fresher. His eyes were blue. His hair had curled, just at the edges.

I drew that man, elbows in, head up, staring straight at his audience, staring straight at me.

*

When the Florentines started to build the cathedral of Santa Maria del Fiore, they didn't have the technology to finish it. The cornerstone, laid in 1296, started a process that wouldn't be completed for one hundred and forty years. Civil war, bubonic plague, and constantly changing architects exacerbated the problem, but it was also something more than that. Builders could create the structure itself, a standard cruciform shape, but not the dome that would span the point where the two halves of the cross came together. No one knew how to bridge such a distance, certainly not with the tools they had.

More than one hundred years after they started, the city held a search for an architect who could solve the problem. Fillipo Brunelleschi, a notary's son, presented theories on how to build the dome. His suggestions were so extraordinary that the board of examiners refused to believe it could be done.

In the end, the city decided to hold a contest. The winner would be the man who could make an egg stand upright. Whatever type of a response they were looking for, Brunelleschi's was certainly unique. Instead of building models or structures to hold the egg, the architect simply smashed the fat end into the table. White and yolk oozed off the table onto the floor. Brunelleschi won the commission.

The reality of his construction was much more than an artistic brainstorm, a flash of showmanship in front of a nominating committee. Even before attempting to build the dome, he had spent years visiting Roman buildings, the Pantheon and the Colosseum, isolating their secrets of proportion and grace. Brunelleschi had done what no other architect had done in modern times, gone back to the beginning to study ancient principles of design.

His model for the dome of Santa Maria del Fiore is still on display in the cathedral museum. His solution to the structural difficulty was to build not one dome, but two. One sat within the other, the first and smaller one supporting the high arching bulk of the second. Laborers stood on the back of what they had built already. The inner dome lifted them weightlessly, to the stars.

Brunelleschi's dome is buttressed by granite ribs that push up and into a marble cupola, the crowning glory on top, where tourists stand and stare at a 360-degree view of the city. Red roof tiles fit together to form armor worthy of a giant. The cathedral defines the city, the way the tower does Pisa, the way the canals do Venice. It determines the come and go of tourists, the push and pull of the streets. Traffic flows around it like rapids around a boulder.

In the days after I first started to sketch, I drew Brunelleschi's masterpiece from every conceivable angle. It took me the better part of a week to come up with scenes I could stand to look at. The first was from directly underneath the dome, done leaning up against a traffic barrier just across the street. The second drawing was from Giotto's bell tower. I climbed the 414 steps and stood at an iron railing, where I was bumped by tourists so often I wasted handfuls of paper. But it was a bird's-eye view, level with the dome just across the way, the red tiles barely out of reach. Children in the cupola waved at me.

The third sketch was from a half mile away, from the Piazzale Michelangelo, where the dome commanded a landscape of medieval towers, the center flower within a stone and water bouquet. The Arno flowed directly beneath my vantage point, each bridge spanning it in three symmetric arches, one after the other, until the buildings gave way to the green of Cascine Park and the river itself twisted out of sight. Graphite seemed wholly inadequate to capture the flood of earth tones, brick, mustard, wheat, and poppy. I went back the next day with my paints.

✳

When I arrived at Piazzale Michelangelo that day, four or five other artists stood at the granite balustrade. They were hard at work, their backs toward the square where the buses dropped off tourists, heads bent toward their papers. There was a similarity to their loose, shabby clothing, their paint-splattered shoes. They had a timeless air about them, as if they had all been standing, silent, painting, for a long time. I joined them without comment, as if there were enough to go around, enough view, enough talent, enough light, as if we were not sensitive to the competition or one another's technical skills. It wasn't until I pulled my hair back that I felt the stares, the glances that made me wrap the rubber band quickly, to drop my arms, taking the emphasis off the lift of my breasts, covering the strip of exposed skin below the line of my sweater. I turned to meet their stares and, like cockroaches scattering at the sound of footsteps, they seemed to disappear, blending back into the landscape, technicians again.

I stayed for the better part of an afternoon, until I had run out of light. I had wet a paper towel with turpentine and was wrapping it around the tips of the brushes when

28

I felt a tap on my shoulder. I turned, expecting to find a Florentine who wanted not so subtly to ask me what time it was, to tell me that he'd seen me staring at him and only wanted to help me with the agony of making the approach.

It was on the tip of my tongue to say the few words that meant "I don't speak Italian" when I realized the man who'd touched me wasn't a stranger at all.

He was the cellist from the square.

"I don't know whether you remember me or not," he said. He wore a navy blazer of some soft material. It brought out the blue in his eyes.

I nodded, then looked down at my paint case, which resembled something a lawyer might carry to work, except it was made of wood, eighteen by twelve by four. In the half of it that came up and stayed open, where businessmen would place folders and sheaves of paper, I kept plates of glass for mixing colors, yellow ochre and titanium white. In the slots where there would be pens, I kept my brushes, different sizes, varying weights. The paints themselves were in the deep well of the bottom, thrown together haphazardly, metallics up against earth tones, primary colors rubbing up against viridian hue.

I couldn't quite focus. One tube of color swam into the other. I slid the clean brushes into their proper places, tucked an extra paper towel into an empty slot. I checked the lids of the paints I had used. It wasn't necessary, but it kept me from staring. It gave my hands something to do.

"I was reading," he said, "on the steps over there? And I saw you."

He had a leather backpack over one shoulder and was wearing the same tweed pants as before. I had imagined him to be Italian, German, Austrian—from a culture that cared about clothing, where tennis shoes were only worn during sports and people actually dressed for dinner. It took three sentences for me to realize he had no accent. That meant he was an American.

"No recitals today?"

He shook his head. "I had work to do."

"Work?"

"Reading." He shifted the weight of his backpack. "I'm a student. At the political science institute." He nodded in a vague direction toward downtown. I had wondered, while I was painting, who lived in those buildings, with their open arched windows and views of the river, the grain yellow facades. I had tried, in my mind, stepping inside of them, crossing a threshold with a book in my hand. "College?"

"Graduate school."

I felt even more awkward then, as if all of a sudden my painting clothes had grown voluminous. And as a matter of fact, they were too big, my comfortable cotton pants, the decrepit sweater of Frank's. Lena had made a face at me when I walked out of the house. Now I knew what she had meant. They were out of place in such a setting, all wrong for a conversation with this man.

"You're an art student?"

I looked up, finally. "Something like that."

"My name is Chad Lesa."

"Joanna Shepherd."

He stood there, hands in his pockets, completely at ease. "I was wondering whether you'd be interested in getting a glass of wine? Or a cappuccino?"

I didn't answer.

"Or maybe I could just walk you down the hill?"

"I don't know."

"You don't know?"

"I'm not very good at these sorts of things."

"What sorts of things?"

Normal things, I wanted to say, common interactions. Interactions that seemed ordinary to everyone else, to people who talked to each other, men and women who smiled and held conversations and didn't find it frightening. I was still trying to manage where I was, where I had found myself, in a world of such richness that my only response was to take peeks at it, to hide in between, licking my wounds.

"I just thought we could have coffee," he repeated. "I promise I'm not an ax murderer or anything."

He shifted his pack again, waiting, and I thought of books and college and all I didn't know, compared to all that this man presumably did. Frank's death washed over me the way it had when Chad had been playing.

I stared at my paint-splattered hands and shook my head.

At the church of Santa Croce, the wooden rafters are painted in bright circus colors, a pattern of lines and circles that dance across the sky. The walls themselves are the color of chalk, appropriate space for marble tombs. Michelangelo is buried there, behind a second-rate monument by his friend Vasari. An elaborate vault for Dante stands empty. The Florentines exiled the famous poet for his political affiliations. When he died, they could not change their minds and get him back. The good citizens of Ravenna refused to relinquish the corpse.

On the floor directly in front of the main altar, flat slabs mark the graves of patriarchs who came before the Medici and gave way to them and the rest of history, ending up with nothing but the great honor of being trod upon, in perpetuity, by tourists on their way to the gift store. Beside the main altar are side chapels, built and maintained for the glory of Florence's ancient nobility, the once-wealthy who lost their fortunes lending to British kings, the once-healthy who ended up black and bloated from bubonic plague. Tourists feed coins into machines that illuminate the remaining pieces of art, the death of Saint Francis, his bodily assumption into heaven.

Silent as usual, I pulled my notebook out of my backpack and squatted down to copy the crest on the Peruzzi family headstone, three pears surrounded by twisting ivy. Before starting, I reached out with one finger to trace the curve of the fruit, as if by touching it I could take it with me, re-create it in a secret garden somewhere, make the original somehow mine. The gray stone felt smooth and cool and silent, as if it had absorbed centuries of conversations by priests and politicians, muted them into nothingness. The light streaming in through the stained-glass windows played tricks with the dimensions, the shadows came and went in a slow heartbeat. I ended up sitting on the floor, legs crossed, hoping no priest would come by, charging me with a sin.

✳

A liver ache is what I said, what I told Lena I supposed I had. I had left a window open overnight. That was my excuse, which was supposed to buy me a day in bed with the shades drawn. Liver aches are sacred in Italy, the ubiquitous illness, the Latin equivalent of a headache. Another landlady would have left me to my misery, but Lena allowed me a mere half day before she brought me a bowl of broth. She laid a hand on my forehead, pursed her lips, and called me a liar. She pulled out my clothes, put my sketchbook and my coat on the table by the front door along with a shopping list.

"What would your grandfather want?" she finally asked, when there seemed no other way to force me to move. She had taken quite a liking to Frank's memory, put a picture of him on the shrine in the living room next to the photographs of her husband, her parents, her absent chil-

33

dren who lived in Milan. She lit candles for all of them every day, prayed to Mary and Saint Maria Goretti, the Sicilian virgin who died defending herself from rape.

"What would he say?" Lena asked again, then put on a recording of Pavarotti and would not let me close my door against the window-rattling swell of his voice.

I put on my clothes and left the house. I didn't know what Frank would want, but death by aria didn't seem likely. I walked, unaware of exactly where I was headed, except away, away from the house, away from myself.

If Chad Lesa had not been playing at the piazza, I might have walked on through the square to the other side of the river or gone to the market and lost myself among colored silk scarves and leather jackets. As it was, I pushed into the knot of people surrounding him and listened to the music that made me want to paint. When he was finished, I threw a few coins into the cello case. They glittered gold and silver against the black felt. Before I even raised my eyes, I knew he would be smiling.

THREE

Artemisia Gentileschi, a Roman woman working during the Baroque period, painted scenes from the life of Judith, a Hebrew heroine. According to an apocryphal story, the Assyrians had laid siege to the Israelite city of Bethulia. The Israelites, believing they were doomed, were on the verge of surrendering when Judith entered the enemy camp and seduced Holofernes, the Assyrian general. After spending days gaining the general's trust, Judith got him drunk, went back to his tent with him, and chopped off his head. At dawn the next morning, she pulled the grisly trophy from a basket and terrified the Assyrians into a screaming retreat.

One of the most famous Gentileschi paintings depicts the exact moment when Judith strikes Holofernes with her sword. She is a big woman, with thick arms and substantial breasts and shoulders. She holds the Assyrian's head in one hand and strains to get the blade *through the sinew and the bone, even though the man is still conscious, even though his blood splatters up in the air and all over her and her maid, who is helping to keep him down on the bed. There is no doubt who will win. Judith does what needs to be done. She will strangle him with her bare hands if she has to—all in the name of God and self-defense.*

※

I park my truck across the street from Rene Riley's diner. Instead of going in right away, I sit there, feeling the weight of the sky through the windshield. The clouds are pulled thin like cotton. I understand how they feel, out in the middle of nowhere, unsure of quite where they're heading.

Bright River appears to have shrunk, mourning better economic times. Main Street looks too narrow, the false front of the old bank building has settled down into comfortable grief. I remember newly painted storefronts, but they are hiding behind sadder versions of themselves. The gilt-edged letters on the post-office window have started to peel. The Gold Delicious Motel burnt down, and where it used to stand is a vacant lot, covered with blue bachelor's buttons and wild sage.

It should not be difficult to cross the street, but somehow it is. Rene has a hand-lettered sign in the window. I stare at it—black felt marker on cardboard—as if it contains a message for me. But all it says is TURKEY SPECIAL WITH FRIES.

Down the street, a black Camaro pulls up in front of the Food Mart. A woman gets out, squints down the street at my truck. She waves, an unashamed motion that uses her whole arm. I do not recognize her or her car, but her welcome pulls me out of my reverie enough to wave back.

A bell rings when I finally push open Rene's door. Lime green vinyl covers the chrome bar stools, pale yellow paint peels from the walls. Black-and-white photographs hang over each booth in a slapdash pattern, a horse-drawn combine next to the 1952 election victory of Bright River's last great mayor. Rene's grandfather is up there, a photograph taken the day he opened the diner, and so is Frank, a town hero after tracking and dispatching a cougar that killed a little boy. The place is smaller and dingier than I remember. It is more precious to me too.

There is one customer seated by himself at the counter, a man in his mid-thirties wearing gray slacks and a tie. His rolled white shirtsleeves reveal pale forearms. He is clearly not a farmer, not even one who is dressed up on his way somewhere.

"Joanna!" Rene squeals when she sees me. Like Chuck, Rene has gained some weight over the years. She's become a mother, her hair a gentle brown instead of the screaming cheerleader blond she dyed it at fifteen. But she smiles at me and it's obvious that the lines the years have drawn around her eyes have come from laughter, not tears.

I walk behind the counter and Rene reaches out to hug me. I tentatively hug back—not knowing quite where my hands should go, over hers or around. She doesn't seem to notice, just folds me into her body as if I am one of her children. Her certainty embarrasses me. It feels as though I haven't been touched in a very long time.

"Sit down." Rene offers me a stool inside the counter, where I can see the grill, the bags full of napkins and paper to-go cups. The man on the other side stops eating, as if he has been waiting for the entertainment to arrive. "Can I get you something?" Rene asks.

"Just coffee for now. Thanks."

She pours me a cup of Maxwell House, smiling. I can see the industrial-sized can under the percolator. *"Acqua sporca"* my Italian friends called American coffee, "dirty water." They've never tasted Rene's, thick and sludge-like, gritty enough to cut holes in the lining of the stomach. It may be many things, but water it's not.

"I have been so jealous of Chuck, seeing you and all, me being stuck either here or with the kids."

The man has curly hair, a broad forehead, a pockmarked complexion. He is clearly listening to every word.

"Thanks for the groceries" is all I can think of to say.

She waves it off. "You have to tell me absolutely everything. It's been so long."

"There's not that much to tell."

"You are a complete and total liar. Chuck says you've been getting the place back in shape."

"Just the front fences. There's a nasty leak in the roof that someone's going to have to look at."

I reach for the sugar. Talking with Rene is like learning to walk all over again. She sets me out at a crawl, sticking to the safety of easy topics. But I watch her and have no doubts that she is merely biding her time before she yanks me all the way to my feet.

"Remember Dan Flood? He did our roof two years ago. Chuck was pretty happy with him."

The man clears his throat and looks pointedly in the direction of his glass, so Rene has no choice but to refill it with lemonade. The brief lull gives him all the opportunity he needs to speak up. "So you're Joanna Shepherd," he says.

I look at Rene. She halfway giggles, as if caught with her hand in the cookie jar. It is obvious she has been gossiping and that I have been the main topic of discussion. "I guess so," I answer.

"Jo," Rene said, "this is Jerry Baker, the new principal at the grammar school."

"It's been three years," he says to her, obviously wanting recognition for time served. Rene shrugs.

"Nice to meet you," I say politely, but really I want to get back to my friend. There are things I had forgotten, the diner and the sight of her face are bringing them back—memories of nights in high school, me and Jack across from Chuck and Rene, years before they were married. We ate thick steak-cut fries, served with brown gravy on the side, planning our escape from this small town.

The principal slides over a seat. "You have quite a reputation as an artist."

Rene laughs. "I'm the one who had the reputation." She pokes at me with a knowing finger, making reference to her own shotgun wedding with such good humor that it is obvious she adores motherhood and her position as Chuck's wife.

"I would've loved to have been here to see you guys get married," I say.

"You should've made the dress."

"Like I know anything about sewing."

Rene slaps me lightly on the shoulder. "It couldn't have been worse than what I actually wore. Yellow. Off the shoulder. I was huge." She makes a motion with her hands. "You'll have to see the pictures."

Jerry Baker tries to reclaim the conversation. "I used to be a painter. Back when I was a vice principal in Portland." He is trying to be charming. It isn't working.

Rene snorts. "You couldn't have been as good as Jo."

He straightens up, offended. "How do you know?"

"Because if you were as good as Jo, you wouldn't be a principal. You wouldn't have been a vice principal. You wouldn't have been a teacher. If you were as good as Jo, you would've been an artist. You couldn't have been anything else."

It is a little over the top, even for Rene, who hasn't seen my work since high school. But there is a hierarchy in small towns. The top of the pyramid doesn't belong to the smartest, or the prettiest, or the ones with the most money, although those things help. At the top of the pyramid are the people who've lived in the town the longest. Rene's family owned the first hotel in town, the best hotel in the county at the turn of the century. In the face of our collective history, the principal doesn't stand a chance.

"Listen," I ask her, "have you ever heard of a woman named Hazel Potts?"

Rene thinks about it for a minute. "Wasn't she that woman who took care of you when you first came to live with Frank?"

And that does it, conjures up an image of a woman in jeans and work shirts, a heavyset woman with a belly and gray hair. She hands me a cookie. She cries on the stairs of the porch, her red lipstick mouth smeared across the back of her hand. The brief memories give me an odd feeling in my stomach, as if a landmark has been moved.

"She's the woman who donated her collection to the library," the principal interjects. "She collected regional history."

"Was that what was in those boxes?" Rene pulls a pad out of her apron pocket. She starts scribbling numbers. "The UPS guy said it took him an hour to get them all into the library."

"Cherry told us all about it at the last school-board meeting," the principal says.

I look at Rene. "Maybe I should go over there?"

Rene slaps the principal's check on the counter. "She's on vacation at Diamond Lake. Be back day after tomorrow."

"She said it has to do with Hazel's will." The principal

pulls his wallet out of his back pocket. "You're one of the beneficiaries."

Rene and I look at each other. Jerry Baker drops four bills on the counter and heads out the door.

✳

When I was small, I hid behind my hair. I hid behind my hair and inside my clothing, squatting on the playground so the hem of my skirt covered my feet. I chewed the sleeves of my sweatshirts, twisted them wet and out of shape with my baby teeth. I ate the dried kidney beans my teacher gave me for counting, made paper-thin molds of my hand out of Elmer's glue.

When I stopped talking altogether, Frank protected me from the neighbors, the women from the church who came right out and told him he should have me tested for retardation. My teacher recommended a psychiatrist. It was Frank's idea to give me finger paints and a rough wall in the barn to paint on. For the weeks I didn't want to talk, no one made me. My grandfather let me take my second-grade class picture with a splash of green in my hair.

I remember every nook and cranny of that silence, every hidden place where my mind wandered unaccompanied by the burden of having to respond out loud. I remember pretending that my mother wasn't really dead. I pretended that something had happened to her, that she was out there, wandering, looking for me. But it was impossible to sustain the fantasy forever. Neighbors were too nosy about it with Frank, and kids were too blunt about it with me. I remember Chippie Stanley, the librarian's son, yelling on the playground, "Your mother croaked!" I also remember being sent to the principal's office for splitting his lip.

∗

Jack Pearce calls at dusk. From my place at the sink, I can see the yellow lights shining in the barn. My hands are wet, covered with the castile soap I use after work. I have to be careful to avoid the blisters where the skin is almost raw, the tender spot between my thumb and forefinger. The soap leaves a faint peppermint smell in the air.

"It's about time." He doesn't identify himself, but picks up the conversation in midstream. He used to do that all through high school, as if I should miraculously know who was on the other end of the phone. Funny thing was, I always did. "I called your number in New York. It was disconnected."

It is strange, after all this time, to hear his voice. It sets up a vibration in my body, the kind of rhythm that spills over into an accelerated heartbeat. It may be love. It may be an anxiety attack. At the moment, it's hard to tell the difference.

"That's true," I manage to answer.

"Since when?"

"It was all kind of sudden."

"Why didn't you tell me you were coming back?"

I am amazed at how simple he is, how he can possibly expect to ask and actually get an answer.

"It's complicated."

He clears his throat. "Did you fly into Seattle?"

"Spokane."

"You could've come into Seattle. Stayed here a few days. I would've driven you home."

"Across the entire state?"

"Of course. And you know it."

I can imagine it, being in the passenger seat of whatever car he owns, insulated by glass and steel from the wind in the mountains, the smell of stockyards in Ellensburg. We would've wound our way over the Columbia River, stopping in Vantage for soft-serve ice cream in flat-bottomed cones. By the time we reached Spokane, it would've been dark. Heading north, I would have fallen asleep, with his square hands firmly on the wheel and music blaring from the tape deck. He would have carried my bags up to the house, been with me when I first opened the door.

"That would've been nice," I say, but there is fear in my voice. I have imagined so many things with regard to him. Very few of them have ever come true.

My grandfather's presence is everywhere in the barn, in the wooden beams of the rafters, in the assorted piles of junk in the corners. Walking into his workshop is like visiting a shrine. He designed it himself, the shelving, the worktable, the doors. He salvaged a bank of drawers from a hardware store in Idaho Falls and kept his tools in them. With the help of Jack's uncle, who did most of the digging for the pipes, Frank put in a sink with cold running water for cleaning and coffee. Some of his mugs are still there, on a bench by the sink, gathering cobwebs.

The room smells of dry wood, old magazines, and rusted metal. Without knowing quite what I am looking for, I begin to dig, pulling boxes off shelves. They reluctantly move, open only under duress, with a slice of a razor blade through duct tape.

I rummage through a carton of fabric and lace and sewing supplies to find a spool of silver wire that looks like Jack's voice. Searching through the shelves in the shop for what I know is there, I pick up stray pieces of wood, stakes for the garden, a piece of porch railing. A set of wooden Coca-Cola crates hides under a box full of odd hinges. A margarine tub holds different sized nails. I pull out a hammer and Frank's power screwdriver, place them on the worktable in a neat row, so they will be there when I need them. A leather punch, stray paint brushes stiff with turpentine, plastic beads—they go in a drawer below Frank's nuts and bolts and washers, where they will be easy to reach.

Before I quite realize it, the split is happening—the split between a picture inside my head and the reality of how a piece will be born through my fingers. Jack's phone call, the sound of his voice after all this time, has sent me through the looking glass. Once I'm there, I don't want to stop, don't want to go back to the other side of the mirror, back up to the house and to bed. My rational mind knows it's late and my muscles protest, but the rest of me would rather stay with the materials that remind me of toys and wordless play, an alternate universe where colors are bright and Chagall bridegrooms are so happy in love they fly. It is the place where I am the most comfortable, the place where I forget.

✳

I wish I could remember the first time I saw Jack Pearce, but I can't. I can see the color of his shirts, secondhand from the Salvation Army in Spokane, pale green with ugly stripes, the way his black hair stuck up in weird ways, the rips in his pants. I can hear the whispers about how tough he was, the rumors about the bite mark on his right biceps—left over from a fight with a seventh-grader in his old school.

But I don't remember his first day in our elementary school, when Chippie Stanley took one look at Jack's dark eyes and dark hair and called him a dipshit Indian fuckhead. Jack, half-Spokane, had never known his father, never lived on the reservation, but he snapped anyway, as surely as if he had been full-blooded and Chippie had been the one to hand out the commodity food. Jack backed Chippie up to the edge of the ravine, threatened to shove him over the edge. They say Chippie almost lost his balance, that the dirt on the hillside crumbled under his feet. Chippie gave up, but when Jack started to walk away, Chippie took a shove at him. Jack whirled around and hit him so hard that Chippie lost one of his eyeteeth.

Because of where we lived, Jack and I rode the school van together, all the way out to the end of the line. On the ride, I tried to read, Grimm's fairy tales and children's versions of Greek myths. But Jack wasn't content with that. He'd pop over the back of the seat to ask what I was looking at. I'd trace the head of Medusa with my finger, he'd pretend to blow his nose in my hair. I'd put my face down close to find every animal hidden in Snow White's jungle, he'd make ape noises in my ear. We'd wrestle, over the back seats of the van, until Mrs. Gillespie, Chippie Stanley's fat married aunt, threatened to pull over.

"I'll tell your parents," she'd warn.

"She doesn't have parents," Jack would say quite deliberately and with a mildly shocked tone in his voice. It got her every time. Mrs. Gillespie would glance back in the rearview mirror to see whether I was visibly upset. I could just catch sight of her worried eyes, her wobbling chin.

47

Then Jack would lick his finger and try to stick it in my ear, and the whole thing would start all over again.

✳

At eleven o'clock, long after I usually go to bed, I am still in my workshop messing around with the wooden crates and the wire and the ivory-colored fabric. I hear the melancholy pull of the train whistle in the distance. Straining, I catch the whisper of the heavy cars, filled with wheat and timber, shuttling down the tracks. It is a lonely, dark sound, a hollow signal of goods going by.

I have flashbacks to elementary-school Saturdays, when Jack and I would lay dimes on the rails, when we spent hours counting flatcars and boxcars, waving to engineers in the caboose. We would stand as close to the tracks as we dared, terrifying ourselves and each other in the forty-mile-an-hour winds howling off the metal wheels and rusted fittings. Then came the search in the gravel for our obliterated dimes, squashed flat and smooth in the silver-gray gravel dust.

Frank had stories of the train, before roads were built and cars took over for horses. He remembered mail delivery when it was twice a week, and the first phone lines in the valley, strung along the barbed-wire fences before there were telephone poles. He talked of party lines and privies and the days before electricity, shooting pheasants when he was eight years old, earning enough money to buy his first pair of long pants.

In other parts of the country, innovation came earlier. Up around Bright River, life had stayed dry and hard and remote long into the Depression. It was a town carved out of stolen Indian land because of rumors of silver and an exaggerated hope of what irrigation could bring.

The reality was that not many people who came during Frank's lifetime made it. Not many of them stayed. But the train still goes twice a day, through town more than to it. It's no wonder the whistle sounds lonely.

FOUR

The Osteria dei Poeti stood at the end of a no-name alley somewhere behind the church of Santo Spirito, in a neighborhood where students dozed on doorsteps, looking up at the sound of footsteps, a swift flutter of their hands hiding the hash. Even in my weeks of walking, I hadn't stumbled into it. The *osteria* posted no menu, had no neon sign out front. It was absent from my guidebooks, because the single view of the river was through dusty windows far in the back. The only indication that it was a place of business was the hand-painted door, the hawk-nosed face of Dante in the upper right corner and a bit of verse in yellow attributed to Cesare Pavese.

Chad pushed open the door, and I followed him down a narrow flight of stairs into a cavernous basement. Warmth filled the plaster vaults, body heat and candles and the open flames of a roasting oven, barely visible in the back, smells of garlic and rosemary rising from peasant dishes and crusty bread.

The bar setup was simple—one tap for beer and a short row of bottles on a glass shelf behind. They had names and colors I didn't recognize, except for the black Jack Daniel's bottle, the green fifth of Tanqueray. The owner, a middle-aged man, called out over the noise of the crowd, greeting Chad like an old friend, reaching across the counter with thick, fat fingers. "Signor Lesa! Pleasure to see you."

"Pino, this is my friend Joanna. She's from America."

"Ah, America!" The man's face lit up and he said something, rapidly, I didn't understand.

Chad translated. "He wants to know if you've ever been to Texas. His second cousin lives in Austin."

I shook my head and Pino raised his hands up, the international sign of futility.

"A bottle of Montepulciano, please. Two glasses."

The man fussed under the counter and Chad searched for a table, but there were none, not even spaces where we might stand.

"Lesa!" A man halfway rose out of his chair. Without rising to his full height, he could clearly be seen above the other students. Chad held up one hand. He smiled and I could tell it had not occurred to him that he would not find a place.

"Walter and I are in school together," he said, sweeping

the glasses off the counter. He nodded in the direction of the table. "Do you mind sharing?"

I shook my head and followed him to the back, around bodies and chairs, through invisible pockets of cologne and sweat.

Chad's friend had taken off his jacket and a sweater, laid them over one of the chairs. His white shirt was open to mid-chest, his collar askew. He gathered up his things as Chad set the glasses down, tucked away a paperback in his leather bag.

"You can't possibly be getting any work done," Chad said. His friend had his own bottle of red wine on the table. It was half empty.

"Not really," the man grinned. "I just pretend."

"Walter Haffner. Joanna Shepherd."

"Nice to meet you," I said. We shook hands. His felt cool, despite the temperature in the room. When he pulled back, I noticed the bones in his wrist, the knot just under his hand, the angular slant to his cheekbones. He was grey-hound-thin, all bone and skin with whip steel muscle.

"So you go to school together?"

Chad looked at Walter. "I'm the one who goes to school. Walter hangs out in the coffee bar on the ground floor of the building."

"Just because I don't like Francini."

"Or Espy or Tolan or any of the others."

Walter turned the bottle around so he could read the label. "A beautiful wine."

Chad poured one for me and one for him, waited to taste his until I had already taken a drink. "Do you like it?" he asked, pulling his chair closer to the table so he could lean in to me, resting his elbows on wood.

The wine prickled my tongue, a taste as strong as espresso, as tart as lemons. "I don't think you should go by me. Where I come from, the wine selection is pretty much limited to Chablis in a box."

"Where's that?" Walter asked.

"Washington state."

"Walter's from New York," Chad explained.

"I've never met anyone from New York before."

"You've got to be kidding!" Walter laughed, as if it had never occurred to him that such a thing was even possible. "What brings you here?"

It was a good question, one that I couldn't answer without telling them much more about myself than I was willing to reveal. I couldn't say I'd run away from home, although that would've been the best answer, the one closest to the truth.

"She studies art," Chad said, which made it sound like I had a teacher. Still, it seemed easiest to agree with him.

"Art is one thing I can confidently say that I know about. One of my mother's hobbies." The way Walter said it made it clear that his mother had many hobbies, expensive ones. Walter glanced at me, a crooked, fleeting little look, as if I had a piece of spinach between my teeth. "Are you any good?"

It was a rare occurrence for me, to hear it couched in

terms like that. I didn't know what he was asking, whether I could draw a realistic representation of a face or whether I'd sold any work. No one had ever paid me for anything, but I had never offered up work for sale either.

"I'm not quite sure," I answered.

Walter waited for me to say something else, but I didn't. That seemed to violate some unspoken rule, because he shifted his weight in his seat and opened his mouth briefly before closing it again. Then he laughed. "Do you have any work with you?"

"Some," I said, but I wasn't sure I wanted to share sketches with him.

"Maybe after dinner. You are here for dinner aren't you?"

Chad glanced at me. "I just invited Jo for drinks."

"Well, in that case, my treat." Walter began clearing his books off the table.

He motioned the waiter over and ordered a full meal. He insisted on paying for it, three courses, no less. It was then that I noticed that his black sweater was cashmere, a rich fabric, soft. I resisted an urge to reach out and pet it.

One or the other of them kept pouring more wine before I had a chance to drain my glass, so it quickly became impossible to tell how much I'd had to drink. I got the distinct impression they liked it that way, keeping me off balance and giggling. By the time the food came, I was famished. Chad and I both ate quickly, willingly, completely. We sucked all the flesh off the bones of the chicken. We left them on a platter in the middle of the table, soaking in a puddle of olive oil and rosemary.

Walter, on the other hand, barely touched his food. He smoked cigarette after cigarette halfway down to the filter, then stabbed them out. They were expensive cigarettes too, Dunhills, imported from England.

"There are lots of things that I can stand in this life," I heard him say, "but Italian cigarettes aren't one of them."

And as pretentious as he seemed, I found myself beginning to like him, beginning to like them both, beginning to like the person I was in their company, shiny, new, and reinvented, without Jack, without Frank, without weight.

They laughed at things I said. It appealed to my vanity more than it probably should have.

＊

After dinner, I handed Walter my sketchbook. He cracked the spine open to the very front, to a point before I had set foot in Italy, some months before Frank's abrupt decline. I had done a series of miniature barns and schoolhouses, each the size of a thumbnail, filled in with colored pencils, brown and white and black. Underneath each one, I had lettered the names of the towns: Steptoe, St. John, McLean. They were small farming communities made up of gas stations and grain elevators, where a rotting center beam in a barn could mean the difference between losing livestock and keeping them, where the choice was between a couple of coats of new paint and food on the table. Food on the table always won.

"Is this where you live?" Walter asked.

"More or less," I said. When Frank could still be left alone, I had taken a driving trip with Jack, around Bright River and farther south, past Spokane and down into the rolling hills of the Palouse, where Jack's older sister lived with her three kids. He'd walked down roads with his nephews trailing behind. I'd sat in the cab of the truck and stared at grain elevators.

Chad came back from the bathroom, his shirt tucked in, an expectant look on his face. "What are we looking at?"

"Just sketches," I said, but Chad moved his chair closer to Walter's so that he could look too. I thought of the margin notes I had written next to particular sketches—Frank's Thresher, Bridge over Bright River. They would know, looking at them, who and what I had loved.

The waiter brought our coffee. He set down three white demitasse cups, a silver pitcher with warm milk, a sugar bowl. Walter did not look up. Instead, with deliberate motions, he turned page after page of my book.

✳

Walter slid the sketchbook across to me without saying anything. The waiter had long since cleared away the dishes, the chicken and the sugar, the milk and the coffee. Walter lit a cigarette before saying anything, drew his knee up to his chest, exhaled hard. A bit of leg showed between the cuff of his dark pants and his slouched black sock. That patch of skin looked sickly pale, strangely unsophisticated.

"You know who this stuff reminds me of?"

"Who?"

"A little bit of Andrew Wyeth, I think, because of the barns and the whole rural setting."

I waited for the punch line, the joke. I didn't think he could possibly be serious. No one in Bright River even knew who Wyeth was. No one but me, no one but Jack because I had made him look at my library books.

Walter took a long drag on his cigarette. "And there's an illustrator—well, he's not just an illustrator. I mean, I consider him an artist, but not everyone does." He blew smoke out of the corner of his mouth. "Anyway, he has a piece with a red fence in it and there's a field and buildings and telephone poles."

"And that's good?" Chad asked.

"I love Ben Shahn. My parents had one of his pieces in their house in the Hamptons."

Chad rolled his eyes, but I could tell by the way Walter said it that he wasn't bragging, not about the art, not about the house where his parents kept it. He sounded almost wistful, as if he might never get to see it again. He tapped his index finger on the cover of the sketchbook. "These are beautiful," he said.

"Thank you."

"No, Joanna." He caught my eye. For the first time all

night, I realized, he was openly looking at me. I had thought, on first glance, that he had blue eyes, but they weren't blue at all. They were gray, the color of storm clouds gathering speed, full to the brim with hail. "Really. I mean it."

"Walter Haffner," Chad said. "I have never heard you give anyone a compliment like that."

"She deserves it."

Chad looked at me. "You know what I think?"

I picked up a stray napkin, began to twist it in my hands. "No, what do you think?"

"The next time someone asks you whether you're good, you should say yes."

I felt so grateful and so homesick that I found myself fighting back sudden tears. Walter put a hand over mine, napkin and all.

＊

They dropped me off at the gate to Lena's courtyard. Chad dug the skeleton key from my bag, slipped it in the lock. Walter kissed me, Italian style, once on each cheek. Chad did the same, but he held my hand a fraction too long. I could almost convince myself I'd imagined it. I must have blushed, because I could feel the heat in my cheeks as I slipped through the door with the promise that, of course, we'd see each other soon.

When I finally made it up into bed, the world spun and sunk in around me as if the mattress were much too soft. I just lay there, half-sleeping, half-dreaming, fuzzy-headed from the wine, thinking of Martin Sheen's character drunk and dancing in the opening of *Apocalypse Now*. I knew it wasn't just acting, that, for realism's sake, Martin Sheen himself had gotten drunk before filming. In the course of the scene, he cut himself with a glass, so up on the screen it was real blood, his blood. I also knew that later in the filming Martin Sheen had suffered an almost-fatal heart attack. Deliberate drunkenness was how it began, the soldier's descent into the underworld.

I knew the risks I was running. Too much wine was an obvious sign that my new friends were nothing but sirens. They would call me with sweet voices, only to crash my ship on the rocks. From the comfort of my bed, I stood on the highest mountaintop and dared the lightning to strike. That night, I thought I could stand up to my own failures, to face the blood lust in the jungle. Retribution was coming. I dared it to take me wherever it would.

My bedroom shades rattled with a gust of wind. I laughed, giddy, because I was arrogant and drunk at the same time, and I was unused to being either one. I turned over on my stomach and, fully clothed, fell asleep.

***

After that first meeting with Chad, that first talk with Walter, the middle portions of days flew by, Italian afternoons passing in a blink. I'd sit at the head of the bed, propped up with pillows, drawing on a pad balanced against my knees. Soft charcoal pencils left wide black lines across the speckled white grain of the paper. The shelves in my room became covered with books and papers, finished drawings and art supplies. I had nowhere to put everything and endangered my own life by stacking it all too high, even on the windowsill, right above my bed.

When it grew dark and I grew tired, after Lena had shut off all her lights and gone to bed, I took to meeting the men at the *osteria*. It was a habit Walter in particular encouraged, plying Chad and me with endless amounts of Chianti and free food. The two of them would talk, arguing politics and philosophy the way some expatriates do, with an arrogance born of distance, a certainty cushioned by the width of the ocean.

While they argued, I would take out my book and try to sketch the objects on the table. I listened to the words fly around me. One phrase from Napoleon sticks in my mind: "The corpse of an enemy always smells sweet." I wrote it down, surrounding it with an intricate design of French bread, bricks of cheese, and miniature guillotines.

During the course of those evenings, I came to know my friends—at least I thought I did, impaired as I was by the shiny haze of alcohol and a decided lack of subjects with which to compare them. Chad, easygoing and congenial, except when it came to matters of his education, where he was competitive to the core. Walter, always in motion, late or leaving or tapping a foot, calling out to the waiter or waving his hands above his head. Chad touched me on the knees, on the shoulder. Walter would tap a cigarette, wailing my name. They both wanted me to agree with them, even when they were on the opposite sides of the fence. In fact, especially then.

*

I wrote Jack letters on fragile blue tissue paper, tiny block letters with sentences in every available space. I filled the margins so I could get away with paying less postage. I slipped in drawings and leaves and the gold-foil wrapper from my favorite type of chocolate.

And my barrage of correspondence yielded nothing in return—not a postcard, not a letter, not a phone call. I blamed it on the Italians, their inefficient mail service and the periodic train strikes. I blamed it on his professors, who were obviously giving him too much work. When it was sunny, I convinced myself that I must have given Jack the wrong address. When it rained, I blamed the weather.

I made excuses for Jack, and I tried so hard to believe them. They were better than the truth, which was that he didn't write and he wasn't going to. My best friend, for some inexplicable reason, had abandoned me.

Walter's family fortune was based on a formula for curing hemorrhoids. It took Walter weeks to actually admit it, and only then when I swore up and down not to laugh. His paternal grandfather, a German-born chemist, patented a family home remedy in the late thirties and licensed it to a company that became a household name on three continents. The licensing agreement afforded the Haffners a percentage of the sales, and residual checks tumbled in for years.

Walter's grandfather invested in real estate, beachfront property on Long Island, apartment buildings overlooking the Sound. He moved his family from the working-class neighborhood where he grew up in Brooklyn to the Upper West Side of Manhattan. By the time he turned forty, he could afford a house in the Hamptons with a Shahn in the bathroom, a Schiele over the fireplace. Walter's father, an only child, inherited it all, the house, the money, and an overcompensating amount of pretension befitting a family only recently rich.

No talking was allowed at the Haffner dinner table. Walter's father brought books to the table and read, Dostoyevsky mostly. The cook served in silence, a soup course, a main dish, a salad, dessert. Walter's mother preferred to sit without entertainment, straight-backed and staring out the French doors of the dining room onto the garden.

As Walter grew older and realized, from lunches at

school and dinner at other people's houses, how much he liked to talk, how much he wanted to talk, he began to resent his father. As a shield against his own anger, Walter began carrying his own books to the table. It was a relief to go to boarding school at thirteen, he said. Eventually, he avoided those dinners altogether by going home with other boys on vacation.

Chad, on the other hand, grew up in a house filled with verbal fireworks. His parents had met in Sienna, where his Italian father was finishing medical school and his Irish-American mother was studying music. It had been made clear to Chad from the beginning that his conception had been a lucky mistake, the result of a broken condom in the back of a Fiat. His father bragged about the event, from the menu at the restaurant that night to the newspaper taped to the inside of the car windows for privacy.

The Lesas had a loud marriage, full of singing and slamming doors. The *dottore* ran an emergency room in an inner-city hospital in Baltimore, and he overflowed with stories of gun-shot wounds and amputations, of a pipe bomb exploding in the men's bathroom. Chad's mother, who answered to Mrs. Lesa at hospital functions but preferred to be known by her maiden name everywhere else, taught at the Peabody Conservatory, part of the music faculty at Johns Hopkins. She needed silence for practice and for her private students. She would yell at anyone in the middle of anything to get it. Chad embraced his Walkman, which shut out the sound of his parents fighting, squabbles over food and entertaining, the disturbing sounds of their exuberant sex.

Summers were spent in the country, in a farmhouse in the hills near Camp David. During school vacations, Chad and his mother lived there. Dr. Lesa came out for weekends and one whole week in the middle of August, when the humidity in the city caused the elderly to faint. During that vacation week, his father wore a straw hat and played at being a country gentleman. He killed snakes and held parties, roasting whole pigs in the stone fireplace behind the house. Chad and his mother played duets on the wide stone porch, their neighbors sitting around them on wicker chairs.

On these long evenings away from the city, away from television and his friends, Chad became obsessed with short-wave radio, on which he listened to conversations from around the world. He practiced Italian and Spanish that way, soaking in news reports he wasn't quite old enough to understand. One summer, he feigned a British accent until his mother grew so tired of it that she threatened to stab him with a dinner fork.

Chad and Walter asked questions of me, the way I had of them. I told the truth. In the telling, it occurred to me that I could lie, that they would never know the difference if I made up a separate life for myself. I could literally be anyone to them; they had no idea to whom I had been born.

But I didn't say much about my mother, about the ways I prayed for Frank to get well, handing him vitamin C almost to the end in an attempt to pretend that he just had a cold. There wasn't time for such morbid topics. We were too busy drinking and laughing and acting as if we were three halves of the same whole.

✳

"I don't believe you can say that about Kissinger," Walter said. The three of us were sitting in the *osteria*, sharing tortellini in broth. It was a rainy day, full of the chill of autumn.

Chad leaned in. "If you take Vietnam . . ."

I interrupted. "If the two of you start arguing about Vietnam, I'm leaving."

Walter finished his soup, sat back, lit a cigarette. He held his arm over the back of the chair so the smoke would drift toward another table instead of toward me. "What better to argue about?"

"She has a point. I'm sure Jo has better things to do than listen to a list of all the reasons Henry Kissinger is a fascist."

"You're both full of it," I said.

Walter put his hand over his heart as if wounded. "Whatever makes you think that?"

"Because you're playacting, just like you were yesterday when we were having that argument about Mondrian." The waiter cleared the soup bowls, brought out thin slices of rare roast beef, seared on the outside with a crust of black pepper.

"Mondrian?" Chad asked. He used the question as a pretext to lean in close to me. For an evening in the *osteria*, it was relatively quiet. Several of the tables sat empty. Chad had more than enough room to stretch out, an aisle where he could've put his legs. He wore a white oxford with thin navy stripes. Even with a candle lit, the scent of food in the kitchen and in our bowls, I could still smell him, the faint hint of musk mixed with the end-of-the-day sweat and oil from his body.

"Piet Mondrian," Walter said. "You'd know if you saw the work. Black lines on white backgrounds. Blocks of color where the lines intersect." He stabbed out his cigarette in the ashtray, took up his knife and fork. "And I still say that he's an important figure in the evolution of painting."

I poured myself another glass of wine. "And I say that you love to argue more than you love art."

"He's a revolutionary figure in the history of abstraction." He held the fork in his right hand and brought the meat to his mouth tines down, European style.

"The paintings don't interest me."

"Have you ever seen one in person?"

"You know I haven't. But I still don't want to have this discussion."

"Well then." Walter looked at me as if his point had been proven.

"Well nothing. The Sistine Chapel? Yes, I think if you saw that in person, full-size, full-color, that would make a difference in your opinion. A bunch of red blocks or yellow blocks or blue blocks, who cares?"

"Careful, Jo, he's getting to you," Chad said.

"Mondrian has no soul. No figures, no eyes, no hands, no soul."

Walter calmly reached over, took my full plate and placed it on his empty one. He began to cut into my dinner with measured strokes. "They remind me of windows. You can look into them and they have this unlimited view. It's pure color, which means pure emotion, and on the other side of the frame—inside the painting—is where everything takes place."

I looked at him. I looked at Chad. Walter raised a piece of meat in the air and nodded, as if he were making a toast. Just when I'd thought he was arguing for argument's sake, he had gone and turned the tables on me.

✴

The next day, I stepped off the bus near the Ponte Santa Trinità. The bridge is one of the most elegant in Florence. The Germans blew it to pieces in the later stages of the Second World War, on their retreat up through Italy. But unlike so many casualties of war, the people of Florence were able to re-create it, collecting the stones from the river and the fragments by the roadside to reconstruct it as it had always been.

Walter was waiting for me by the statue of Spring, an allegorical figure matched by the three other seasons on the other corners of the bridge. Spring was special, though, the most ravaged by enemy assault. She'd lost her entire head during the bombing and had been without it until a fisherman downriver had pulled it whole out of the river, the white of the marble in contrast to the mud at the bottom of his net.

Walking on the narrow sidewalk that ran next to the river, behind a tourist couple in Bermuda shorts, I watched Walter pacing, short steps back and forth, moving to protest that I was late. With her head firmly on her shoulders, Spring stared out over the traffic on the bridge, keeping watch on Walter until I reached his side.

"Finally!" he virtually yelled. "What took you so long?"

We had made plans, over the phone, to meet, but he wouldn't tell me why. He had simply demanded that I be there. "Bus got caught in traffic. What's your hurry?"

He looked at his watch and began to walk, taking long strides down via Tornabuoni. I had to take two steps for his every one, to keep up with his pace and the length of his legs. "It's just that Paolo's expecting us."

"Who's Paolo?"

"Paolo Fiore. Friend of mine. He owns a villa here downtown."

"Jesus, Walter. Where do you meet these people?"

Walter wasn't about to answer. He had a private life that I was just beginning to glimpse, a host of acquaintances

I had never met, certain parties to which neither Chad nor I was invited. We speculated that it had something to do with his money, a social circle from which we would always be excluded.

Walter took a breath, as if he had to explain a difficult concept to an already restless child. "Here's the deal. At the turn of the century, Paolo's villa was a sanatorium for wealthy British ladies who wanted rest cures. In the last twenty years or so, it's been completely renovated, turned over to studio space."

"And?"

"Well. It's not exactly his building. But Paolo manages the civic group that owns it. You see, the city wants to cultivate the idea that Florence is a living artistic community, not just a place that houses a lot of dead art. And it's this man who decides pretty much who gets to work there. He likes foreigners. Avant-garde stuff. Especially unknown Americans."

"Really?"

"To be honest, he likes Czechs better, Poles. Eastern Europe and oppression. Better press. But Americans are fine. I told him I'd subsidize the rent if you got a space. It's a year lease, culminating in a group show. Some publicity. He said he had something on the third floor. He wasn't even sure if he should award it this go-around, because it's small and the windows are bad. They've had some problems with the heating system."

"You've got to be kidding."

Walter stopped in front of a square building with thick rough stones on the ground floor, metal rings for tethering horses, wrought-iron holders for torches and lamps. "Yes, this is all just an elaborate joke." Walter looked at his watch. "We're supposed to be inside by now."

"How much is this subsidy, exactly?"

"About six hundred dollars a month."

He acted casual, as if he gave away that much money all the time. And maybe he did, dropping it here and there at dinner as if he never gave a thought to how much it was or where it was going. But bundled up, all in one amount, a monthly stipend not tied to his pleasure or survival in any shape or form, had to be unusual, even for him. Not even Gatsby threw parties out of sheer generosity.

"Why would you do this for me?"

Walter looked at me. "Investment purposes. I give you space, you give me a painting. In three years, I sell it for fifty thousand dollars."

"Bullshit."

"You're a Georgia O'Keeffe. I'll be Stieglitz."

"We're not sleeping together."

"Obviously." He said it with such a dry-martini voice that I had to laugh.

"Seriously. I just have a hard time believing that anyone would do this for me."

A woman in furs walked by, leaving a trail of perfume in her wake. "You don't get it, do you?"

"No, I don't."

"Your work"—Walter paused, as if considering how to articulate something he'd never quite said—"is remarkable."

"So is a lot of other people's."

"You don't understand." He leaned up against the wall. "It sets off bombs in my head. It makes me feel like someone is inside my head with a crowbar, forcibly expanding my skull. You do things I wish I could. You make pictures I need to have."

I could hear the truth in his voice, the tightness in his chest giving way to a red wash of emotion, and I had to look away, to stare at his feet and the cement of the sidewalk, the gold-foil glitter of chocolates in a nearby window. If I'd caught his expression, it would have been too much.

"I want to make it possible for you to keep doing whatever it is you want."

I wrapped my arms around his waist, pressed my cheek into his chest. I had thought that without a family there would be no one to look out after me. I felt as if Walter, that afternoon, had gone a long way toward proving me wrong.

FIVE

The summer I turned thirteen was scorching hot, so hot that by mid-June the weeds along the riverbank had withered, dried up, and died. By July, the state had to fly in smoke jumpers from Colorado and Montana to attack the forest fires.

It was a mile from the farm to the river. Jack and I were walking along the railroad tracks, towels around our necks. I regretted the fact I hadn't worn socks. My heels felt raw from the rub of my tennis shoes. Underneath my overalls, my new bathing suit scratched in all the wrong places.

Jack balanced on the rails, one foot in front of the other like an acrobat, eyes focused straight ahead. I walked behind him, taking exaggerated steps to stay on the ties. From time to time, he took a look back to make sure I was still following.

We passed the warning signs on the way to the bridge: DANGER in big red letters and NO TRESPASSING accompanied by the threat of jail time, or $500, or both. Jack cracked his towel like a bullwhip and hit the sign on his right with a resounding snap. We knew the schedules as well as the conductors. Freight traveled southwest in the morning. People traveled northwest after dark. Two trains a day.

Jack loved to stand on the bridge, on the very edge on the wrong side of the guardrail, daring anyone who came along to jump. It was an abrupt and terrifying drop into the swimming hole, and there was always the threat of being swept downriver, smashing into boulders, or being sucked into the power turbines, spit out as fish food underneath Bright Sun Dam. If it came right down to it, Jack always said, he'd rather face mutilation in the turbines than paralysis on the river bottom. "That way I could wave my stumps in everyone's face," he boasted.

Jack had been planning to go swimming since the first thaw in April, when the crocuses cut through the melting snow. But we hadn't made it. In the spring, rough winter weather kept the water too wild, even for Jack, and once it hit summer, word had already gotten around that Jack's mother had caught him hitchhiking out of town after buying Drum tobacco and rolling papers. Frank, neither a stupid man nor a careless guardian, kept me pretty busy on the farm for a few weeks after that.

The water was a muddy green that day, slow-moving and languid. The algae smell was so thick I could taste it. As we stepped onto the bridge, the ground fell away. The ties were evenly spaced and sturdy, the way they had been over land. There wasn't room for my body to slip through, even if I somehow fell. But that fact didn't reassure me. The air under the bridge felt sinister. The water was waiting to swallow me whole.

When we reached the middle of the bridge, Jack shucked off his thongs, clambered over the guardrail as if his body had been designed to do that one thing. "C'mon," he said, but I didn't move. It was too far down.

"You go first."

"Let's go together."

"I don't think this is a good idea."

"That's your grandfather talking. Chuck did it yesterday. No brain damage."

"With Chuck, how can you tell?"

"Ha ha ha." Jack held onto the guardrail with one hand, facing the water. I could see a barely perceptible shake of his head. Then he bent his knees. Like a diver off a springboard, heading into a crystal-clear chlorinated pool, he jumped out and down and all the way away. I felt my stomach go with him.

He hit the water with a loud splash. Within seconds he surfaced, whooping with the sudden chill. It looked simple when he did it, but I wasn't convinced.

"Are you okay?"

"It feels great!" he yelled to me, treading water. "C'mon."

I unbuckled the tops of my overalls and let them fall to

the ground. Even with the heat, I got goose bumps, a prickling rash over my legs and my newly developed chest. I could feel the skin stretched across my collarbone.

Jack swam with a self-taught stroke to the shore, clambered up the bank, picking his way carefully through the dry money plants. If I waited, he would be beside me, up close, all the way there to watch me being awkward. To avoid that, I hoisted myself up over the guardrail, putting my hands where his had been.

I couldn't look any farther down than my feet, than the old dry wood of the bridge. I wondered what would happen if I got splinters, whether my toes would get infected. It was better to imagine gangrene than the jump. I held on to the railing so hard my fingers hurt.

"Nice suit," Jack said. He had shaken his hair and it stuck out in strange points, like a freshly washed dog.

I looked down at my body and all I could see was bare flesh, not even white but pink, blemished, prickling. He, in turn, was nut brown. "New," I mumbled.

Jack shrugged, but stared a minute too long at my chest. He seemed to be on the verge of asking when it got so big. I wouldn't have known how to answer. "You ready?"

"I don't think so."

Jack climbed over the railing to stand next to me.

"What are you doing?"

"Jumping," he said.

"Get away from me."

"Give me your hand."

"No."

Jack poked me in the arm. "Stop being such a baby. I'm going to count. And on three we're going to jump."

"Jack."

"Look straight ahead." He grabbed my hand. "Pick a spot on the bank."

"I don't want to die."

"See that break in the ridge? Stare at the big outcropping. All the way down."

"Tell me I'm not going to die."

"Keep staring at the rock. Make sure your legs are together and your arms are tucked right before you hit."

"I can't."

"You've done it in the pool. You're fine. One." He squeezed my hand tightly. "Two." I stared at the rock, straight at it. It had smooth edges, as if it had been there for centuries, waiting. "Three."

Jack swung the hand that held mine up and out. He dragged me into the air.

The falling lasted an instant and forever both. The opposite bank of the river moved, the trees and the hillside fell with us, a wicked blur of deep green-gray and brown that told me I was moving impossibly fast. Jack let go. The water, when I hit, sucked me down, cold and oblivious to my screams.

It clung to me with whispers of sea and mermaids at once golden and muddy, so muddy my legs hit dirt, but not bottom, then fear seized me again, not the same fear as when I tried to twist up the courage to jump, but a primordial fear of darkness and ooze and not knowing what might grab me. On the heels of fear came the overwhelming need to breathe, and my legs began to kick until up and up I came, breaking the surface of the water. Once in air, I gasped, my arms and legs treading water, until I heard Jack laughing and the world came into focus and I knew I was alive.

*

For my birthday that year, Frank bought me an anatomy book, a college text, fat with drawings and X rays. The illustrators had cut the skin open, then peeled it back. There were two or three views of the same area, first with an overlay of fat, then with it scraped away to reveal the organs, the pink appendix, the sinister brown colon.

I stared at that book for hours and couldn't work my mind around it all, how the muscles attached to bones, how the bones attached to one another. I tried to produce sketches from the glossy pages, but got caught in the section on the reproductive system, imagining skin I had never seen. The realities of the human body defeated me.

*

Every morning, I go down to the barn as if I know what I am doing, but in reality I have no idea. After the initial burst of energy on my return to Bright River, my creative work has stopped. It is as if a drain has been plugged. In the sunlight of early autumn, I sit stagnant, fetid and brown. I stare at my materials, arrange my paints in rainbow rows, heft the spool of silver wire, waiting for it to speak to me.

I refill my room gradually. It might go faster if there were more of me, but each load of boxes means a walk with a dolly from the barn to the house, a trip or two or three up and down the porch stairs. None of the boxes is marked, and each time I cut through the silver duct tape, I am surprised. Dishes go in one room, books in another. I leave my old clothes in boxes in Frank's old bedroom. I wear his flannel shirts with the sleeves ripped short, pajama bottoms with masculine checks and stripes. Someone used to live in the layers of my old sweatshirts and jeans. I'm not her anymore.

I leave the barn, step out to the garden. By the looks of it, no one has planted for two or three years. Morning-glory vines have taken over, snaking their way up poles that someone hammered into the ground for snap peas. Raspberry bushes have gone wild and leggy, too tall to have berries anymore.

I walk back inside. The air feels dry, surfaces wooden beneath my fingers, as if I am standing inside an empty seedpod. I come and go as if through mouse holes.

❋

I make it to the library at three o'clock. The elementary school, across the street, is letting out for the day. I stop in the middle of the block for the sixth-graders with red plastic flags, watching them help the five- and six-year-olds cross the street. One girl trails a doll by her foot. I wonder whether she brought it for show-and-tell.

My window is rolled down and I can hear the voices of the mothers who tuck their children into cars and belt them safely in. One woman grabs a boy by the elbow. "Where's your sister?" she hisses in his ear. He bites his lip and lowers his eyebrows against her. He does not even like his sister, those eyebrows say, so why should he be yelled at just because she is late.

A few children trudge up the library steps in front of me. They hold the heavy oak door open without meeting my eyes. Inside the building, the smell is the same as I remember, a blend of dry paper and dust. Sound is swallowed up by a heavy carpet.

I ask the high school student behind the main desk where I might find Cherry Stanley and I am directed to her office, down the hall, in between religion and biography. As I enter the room, the woman is sitting behind her desk. She uses half glasses to see a row of figures. She wears a velvet pantsuit the color of Hershey's chocolate, her hair dyed and styled to look like Jacqueline Onassis.

I clear my throat. It is strange, how quickly I have become ten years old again. It's been a long time since I hit her son Chippie, but I expect to be met with disapproval anyway.

Mrs. Stanley looks over her glasses. "Jo Shepherd." She puts the paper down on her desk.

"Mrs. Stanley." I am not comfortable calling her by her first name. I never did before. She does nothing to encourage me in that direction.

"Hard to believe after all this time." She purses her lips. It is clear from her expression that she has written me off, the way she has probably written off Jack, and Chippie himself. Especially Chippie, who, according to Rene, lives in Chicago and makes a good living trading agricultural futures. In Mrs. Stanley's opinion, we have all turned our backs on her town in favor of fleeting opportunities and the company of idiots. None of us has much of a right to come back.

"You wanted to see me?"

"You've heard about Hazel."

"I think so."

"Let me show you what we're talking about."

Locking the office door behind her, Mrs. Stanley leads me past all the STAFF ONLY signs, down into the subbasement, where the walls and floors are unfinished, where the lightbulbs burn bare. There are cartons there, dozens of them, stacked one on top of another.

"We put them down here when they first arrived. We didn't know exactly how long it would take to get ahold of you. Of course, it made it much easier that you came home." She glances at me sideways, as if expecting me to do something disruptive and startling. "The collection has the potential to be quite a resource."

"What is it exactly?"

"I thought someone would have told you by now."

"Actually, they respected your right to do the honors."

"For once!" She smiles for the first time since I arrived. It softens her features considerably, makes me wonder what she'd look like with her own hair, instead of Jackie's.

"Well. Hazel Potts was a photographer. She set up shop with her husband Elmer in the mid-thirties. His collateral paid for the studio, but she was the talent. It was clear from the beginning that she had an eye for capturing life out here. He was better at simple things, portraits, school pictures. But she was the real artist. She also collected regional paraphernalia, glass photographic plates from people's basements, letters, scrapbooks, that kind of thing.

"Elmer had a heart attack in the early seventies and there was some talk then of her donating the materials to the library, but she decided to take it all with her when she moved down to Phoenix. It has the potential to be a real treasure for us, especially given the explosion of research into Western women lately. Hazel was quite unique for her time. Two historians from the University of Washington have already called."

Mrs. Stanley is clearly proud of the possibilities, but I still don't understand what they have to do with me. "Jerry Baker said I'm in the will?"

An odd look passes over her face. It is just a flicker, somewhere around her eyes. If I didn't know better, I would imagine she is hurt.

"You have the right to look at the collection first.

Anything you want to keep in your personal possession is yours. Anything that you don't remains here."

I glance at the stacks and stacks of material. The cartons are not marked, except for address labels that direct them to the library. They seem identical, just big enough for file holders, eight-and-a-half-by-eleven-inch sheets of paper and an odd manila envelope. "So I could take it all."

"Yes. You could." She says this as certainly as if I will. She holds it against me, the lost time, my undeclared length of stay. It is as if I am flirting with someone she loves.

"How long have you know about this?"

"A few weeks. We were trying to get ahold of you."

She is defensive, but I'm not implying that I should have been contacted sooner. It's just that she seems to have jumped to a number of conclusions in a very short time. She thinks she knows me, but she does not.

"Do you have any idea why she would do this?"

"I suppose she imagines it has some historical value."

"Why me? Why did she offer it to me?"

Mrs. Stanley pauses, choosing her words carefully. "She probably hoped you had grown up into the kind of person who would want it."

❊

The summer I was sixteen, Frank paid Jack to work for him. Together, they put a new roof on the barn. I offered to help, but Frank said I was too important to him.

"Let the hired help break his leg," he said. But he said it with a wink because by sixteen, Jack had fallen in love with Frank, the way young men do with older brothers or with sports figures. During the school year, Jack came over to study with me, but ended up working with Frank, fixing the washing machine or siphoning oil mixed with gas into the chain saw, hero worship in his eyes.

They worked on the roof, protected with harnesses and a series of ropes, a system Frank had used climbing mountains in the decade after the war. Shirtless and sweating, they took refuge in the house during the heat of the day. They pulled up sections of weathered cedar shakes, dropping them three stories to the ground. I raked up the pieces, for birdhouses and kindling, to be somewhere near them as they walked in the sky. I tied tar-paper bundles to the ends of rope and hoisted them over pulleys into the air, as they walked like giants on steeply sloping eaves.

Frank passed the working hours with stories of altitude sickness and glaciers. It had been forty years since his ascent of Rainier, his explorations of Mt. Baker and Desolation Peak, but he called them forth on those hot afternoons as if he could still feel the bite of the snow. He argued that it had been dangerous, but Jack didn't believe him. Jack was too strong, too sure of himself and his own abilities. At sixteen, he didn't understand how easily it could all go wrong.

But Jack learned, that summer, when he blithely unclipped from the safety line to reach for a thermos of lemonade. It was only an extra two feet away, he said later. He got his drink, but then somehow lost his footing. He would've fallen if Frank hadn't already been in motion toward him, if he hadn't caught him by the wrist and held him securely. I could see them framed against the noonday sky, Icarus endangering his father by flying too close to the sun.

"It only takes one accident," Frank said, and he sent Jack home to think about it. My friend came back the next day and strapped himself in, more dependent on my grandfather than ever.

※

According to the church, I was supposed to wait until I got married to have sex. It was one of those rules I said I didn't believe in—in high school, listening to other girls talk about being felt up in the backseat of cars. I thought to myself there was no way I'd wait to sleep with Jack, if he asked me. I would never hold back if he showed any indication of wanting me.

But I realize now that I would've been willing because it was not really about sex, not about how good it felt. If Jack had wanted to sleep with me, I would've been eager because it meant he cared for me. There was no doubt in my mind that I would've slept with Jack before we got married, but—more insidiously and never quite spoken—there was also no doubt that if we did sleep together, then that meant we were in love, the kind of love that led to a white dress and cake at the reception.

I'll give Jack credit for knowing me better than I knew myself. I never said a word about any of this, didn't even quite realize I felt that way until years later, when my perceptions shifted. But on some level Jack must have known what intimacy meant to me, how desperately I wanted it from him. He never offered anything he couldn't take back, never promised anything he didn't mean. He had a certain kind of vision, the one that saw the thin string attached to me, red and trailing in my footsteps.

❋

I drive to the cemetery. It commands a prominent place in town, on the hill behind city hall. There is no one around, so I lie back across Frank's grave. My hands reach out, forming a cross that touches the graves of my mother and grandmother too. I stare up at the trees. The big maple has begun to turn and the late-afternoon sun shines yellow through the red, turning it liquid against the sharp blue of the sky. I pray to God or talk to Frank, I'm not sure which. The words just come and I say them out loud because there is no one else to hear me, no cemetery at all, no other visitors, just me and the grass and the ground and the cold air. I beg the sky to tell me what to do, how to stop the buzz inside my head, the ringing in my ears.

I turn over and lay my face on the grass. I wonder what it will be like to be dead. I imagine heaven on top of the clouds, a place where no one will ever think I'm odd or unlikely, where I will never think those things about myself. In heaven, there might be cemeteries, but instead of stones, they will be full of flowers. The dead will move through them, disembodied, light. They won't have the weight of a fleshy self from which to emerge, an uncertain layer of fat and skin.

My fingers turn red with cold. The grass leaves an organic pattern on my cheek. I whisper secrets to the ants. I have fallen so far inside myself that I ask Frank how I am supposed to find my way back. I picture myself spinning, sowing seeds over all of the graves. Fragile and brilliantly colored, flowers would make more sense than the short grass. There is nothing so manicured about the death in my life.

Leaving the cemetery, I don't use the road. Instead, I break a trail through the trees down to the parking lot. I step on ferns, dying back in the cool of autumn, the odd dry branch cracking underfoot. It is like dusk there, under the canopy of the trees, almost brisk enough for thermal shirts and wool socks. Underneath one ponderosa pine, I find two owl pellets, slick and matted balls, regurgitated bits of undigested prey. I keep my eyes on the ground and have put two pellets in my pocket before I reach the truck.

At home, I set the pellets in the microwave and heat them until they are completely dry. It kills the bacteria and makes excess material easier to remove. Then I dissect the pellets with tweezers. They smell like nothing, dry feathers and a bit of extra dust, but the scraping reveals bones, the ankles and ribs and jaws of unfortunate mice. I clean them using a bit of soft cloth and dishwashing detergent. They turn out to be the same bleach white of the Lifesavers I pulled out of the glove compartment of Frank's truck. Setting them out on paper to dry, I imagine the animals they used to be. I wonder what kind of wire God would use to fasten them back together.

✳

When handling Hazel's collection, I wear thin cotton gloves. They come a hundred to a box, with no right or left or individual size. By the end of the day, when I discard them, they are black at the tips. I am proud of my gloves in a weird sort of way—I take them off carefully so that they retain their shape. I stand them up on top of unopened boxes when I leave.

Hazel has left few clues as to what I am doing here, so I sort the photographs into piles, marked and unmarked, identified and not. It is good that no one uses the subbasement for anything else, because the spread overtakes the table by the middle of the second afternoon. I use the floor and the top of the file cabinets for everything before 1900, views of town celebrations taken from the roof of an old hotel. The exotic competes with the mundane, the arrival of a barnstorming team with a cat curled on a front porch.

Through photographs, I am introduced to Hazel and her husband: Hazel and Elmer in front of their store, Hazel and Elmer standing by a car with a rounded hood and enormous bumpers. It becomes apparent that they did not have children—in every picture it is only one or the other or both of them. Elmer reading his paper, Hazel with her camera. Overweight and ready to please, Hazel smiles widely for posed pictures. She has full cheeks and deep dimples, long hair swept back off her face. But when she is caught in the course of things, moving from one place to another or looking up from the camera as she's putting in film, Hazel Potts has quite another expression, one of annoyance, as if she does not like to be taken by surprise, as if she has better things to do with her time. It must be Elmer who intrudes on her, waiting in doorways to catch her unaware. Her expression makes it clear that she doesn't like him sneaking around. Maybe, just maybe, she doesn't like him at all.

In other boxes, I find memorabilia, scrapbooks kept by ladies, clippings from newspapers, records of births. One is an album of death, cards of sympathy and condolence pasted onto black pages as carefully as if they had been markers of a joyful event. There are those too, wedding albums full of cards with roses on the front, ribbons woven through the edges. There is one whole box devoted to the dance hall.

One carton takes me back to the beginning, when roads were nothing more than worn ruts between fields, and barbed-wire fencing cost more than building a whole barn. On top of the photographs lies a sheet of paper, a map of the town as it appeared at the turn of the century. Streets are laid out in a grid pattern, buildings numbered and identified in a key that runs down the right side of the paper. Coordinates show the boundaries of plots of land, homestead sections and the cemetery on the hill. Our family name is penciled in, exactly where it should be.

✳

Walter always tried to argue that there was no American cuisine. If I could, I would track him down, sit him at Rene's counter, and force him to try one of everything on the handwritten laminated menu, starting with the lumberjack hotcakes and ending with the roast beef and mashed potatoes, topped off by hot apple pie with a scoop of soft-serve vanilla ice cream. With his eyes glazed over, he'd be forced to concede.

Jerry Baker is sitting at the counter of the diner when I walk in to pick up my club sandwich. I can't eat in the archive, but it is good weather and I would rather park my truck on the hill then sit inside all day. Rene has the sandwich all ready in a white paper bag, but Jerry makes a show of taking a napkin out of the holder and wiping down the seat next to him. In the time since I have been home, I have run into him almost every other day. His charms have already worn incredibly thin.

"Sorry, Jerry. Getting this to-go."

"Haven't seen you much." He stares at me, the kind of

look that lasts a hair too long. I am hardly looking my best in jeans and a flannel shirt, but I am single and under fifty.

"I've been busy."

"What are you working on?"

Rene, lurking behind the counter so that she can eavesdrop, makes a show of dumping the coffee grounds into the garbage. She measures out a new pot, jams the basket back in the machine.

"Bones," I answer, because it is the truth. "I am making marionettes out of them."

That puts him off his stride. "Well." He makes a valiant effort anyway. "I was wondering . . ."

Rene knows good and well what is happening, interrupts him midsentence to ask me whether I want chips with my sandwich.

"Actually, do you have any cookies?"

"There's this place down on the highway," he continues. "They have bands on the weekends. Not a bad steak, either. If that ever sounds good."

"Maybe," I answer.

Rene's shoulders shake as she slides two chocolate-chip cookies into a plastic bag.

✳

At home, I fill a bucket full of hot water and dishwashing liquid. I get down on my hands and knees with a hard-bristled brush and scrub my kitchen floor in search of memories. I know Hazel Potts is here, somewhere in this house, somewhere deep inside my head, and I aim to find her. I feel like I have a piece of hard candy stuck in my windpipe. I want to be able to breathe.

With my pants wet, the muscles in my back warm from effort, I dig my way into corners, into hard-to-reach spots under the cabinets. I dump the dirty water into the sink, fill the bucket a second time. I slosh suds over the seams, the cracks in the linoleum where particles of food have collected. I obliterate bits of stuck-on, ground-in grit. I rinse the bucket and fill it a third time. And that is when it comes, up and out, from the center of my stomach into the hot water. I hear Hazel's voice, level with my ear. She stands behind me, one hand on my shoulder, the other hand holding out a canning jar for me to admire. There are others, gleaming clean on a dish towel on the counter, crystal-clear. The one she holds in front of me is special, though, the color of blue sky. The room is warm, full of steam and the smell of ripe peaches. Isn't it pretty, she asks me in a whisper, as if it is a secret she wants to keep from Frank. We stand in the kitchen, an orphaned five-year-old and a sixty-year-old woman, worshiping at the altar of a blue bell jar.

SIX

Paolo Fiore handed me the key to the studio
and tactfully closed the door behind him. I slipped the key
into my pocket and turned to take in the off-white walls,
faded with time and age to the buff gray of oyster shells. The
floor was the same color and uneven. I took an orange out of
my bag, set it down along the wall by the door. It slowly but
surely rolled to the other end of the room, nestled in among
the pipes under a stained industrial-sized washbasin.

I opened the bank of four windows and folded back the
shutters. Over the sink was another window, cracked and
dusty, from which I could see into the building next door,
which was under renovation. Scaffolding covered the front
and the side of it.

The interior of the door had been painted blue by

someone who had come long before me. That color made me see gold stars where there were none, a fiery comet hurtling past the cold atmosphere of earth. In the corner, a steam radiator made strange noises, the pops and gurgles of a surly animal's digestion.

There was nothing in that room, no furniture, no ghosts, nothing but the sound of the radiator and the rise and fall of my own breathing. I blinked, half-expecting to find myself back at Lena's with my wardrobe doors open and clothes all over the floor. What I saw was my orange, what I saw was mine and mine alone, four blank walls and a ten-foot ceiling.

I searched through my coat pockets and found a length of string, a thumbtack, a pencil stub. I took off my shoes and, in stocking feet, I measured out the room. At the center, I stuck the thumbtack in one end of the string and pushed it into the floor. I wound the other end around the pencil and pulled it taut. Each move I made disturbed a puddle of dust. Using the string like a protractor, I drew a perfect circle.

Then I lay down in the middle of that circle, arms outstretched, the model of Leonardo da Vinci's sketch of the perfect proportions of man. Steam rushed into the radiator. I acknowledged heat as the source of life and prayed for my own soul, that I might be cared for, that I might be blessed. I felt the laying-on of hundreds of hands.

With each breath, I felt the grief begin to leach out of me, each drop filtered through my skin. The Virgin didn't come, as I might have wished, to mark the moment when I began my new life, but she sent the memory of lilacs and the sweetness of picking them as a child, of being small and sweet and sure of myself.

*

I didn't tell Lena about the Virgin Mary, but that doesn't mean she didn't suspect. Each Sunday, she took me to her church, with its amber windows and incense smell. It felt like a womb there, dark as it was, warm with life. I can still see the side chapels with their layers of aging paint, the peeling faces of saints and angels, marble altars glorifying patrons long since dead. Wrought-iron candle holders in front of the altar to the Virgin supported a hundred flickering yellow flames. Heavy coins dropped one by one into the metal box marked OFFERINGS. Young people wandered in, still wearing Saturday-night black.

Lena never asked me to believe, but she must have known that I already did. She was the one, back in the apartment, who clucked her tongue and pulled out a catalog of the *Lives of the Saints*, handed me money to run down to Feltrinelli's, the bookstore with a good English-language section, to buy the best dictionary I could find. When I protested, she insisted, pushing two pink bills into my hand, almost one hundred dollars, as if she were my mother and I had shown up at a family wedding wearing the wrong shoes.

"Tomorrow," she said in Italian, "you will buy the dictionary. Tomorrow, you will start to read." She pointed at me with a lumpy, arthritic finger. "You will find it interesting."

Lena stared me straight in the eye. I had no choice. In an earlier age, she would have been Elizabeth, she would have been Ruth, a companion during hardship, a prophet of things to come.

✳

At Cascine Park, overlooking the river and under a canopy of elm trees, there was a market every Tuesday. It wasn't for tourists, but ordinary Italian women looking for bargains. Vendors arranged white tents on either side of the wide cement walks, filled them with sweaters and shoes and kitchen goods, with silver-edged mirrors and gold jewelry.

The first thing that caught my eye there was an elderly lady who tottered past wearing a full-length mink and heels too high for her uncertain balance. She carried a brown terrier under her arm. The animal had a pouting expression, a tiny yapping mouth. Three girls brushed past her, giggling, teenagers in tight black miniskirts and high platform shoes. They all had long hair pulled up in plastic clips, fastened back with bows. They wore too much foundation, trying hard to hide their acne scars. One of them wore hoop earrings that reached her jawline. Another cracked gum. The third used a mirror in one of the booths to reapply her lipstick, a bright fire-engine red.

I sat down on the pavement, off to one side, and began to draw the faces of those girls, working quickly before they made their way past me, along down the market line. I regretted losing the matron, regretted losing the dog.

Each time I looked up, I saw more eyes, more clothes, more women, an overweight lady selling ties, a middle-aged clerk in the bar kiosk, the one with the paper apron and paper cups, handing out single shots of espresso. There may have been men there, but I didn't see them, didn't care what they looked like, didn't care where they were. I focused on curves and shoes, practical coats and wedding rings. I imagined pregnancies and failed love affairs, secret screams and a world inside each one, a world like the one inside of me.

By the end of the day, when the vendors packed up their carts, driving small trucks up onto the sidewalk to haul them away, my book was flooded with these women, a wave of female strangers, an ocean of half-finished faces, hiding behind their mermaid hair.

※

Walter played soccer at the fields up the road from the market square. He played midfield, sometimes up and sometimes back, almost always clashing on the sidelines, forcing an aggressive opponent either out of bounds or into a mistake. He attacked the game with single-mindedness, an expression of intense, almost violent concentration.

His aim was to stop, to thwart, to kill the forward trajectory of the ball, and he would throw his head, his chest, his knees, his feet into the way. His teammates called him a murderer. The other teams called him worse.

After games, Walter gave me rides home on his motor-cycle, a sleek red Kawasaki, which dwarfed the Italian scoot-ers. Walter drove as if life held absolutely no meaning. He talked over his shoulder at forty-five miles an hour heading into a traffic jam on a crowded street. When I dug my fin-gers into the loose skin around his waist, he only yelled at me to stop worrying. We flew past cars in a flurry of honks and yells and metal bumpers. I never got over the fear, the terror of Italian traffic, riding without a helmet. I put my head in his shoulder to hide my eyes. Better to turn away from death than stare it head-on.

That afternoon, after the market, there was a problem with his bike. Walter had grunted at me when I arrived, bent back down, intent on fixing it. I stood there, backpack over one shoulder, hands in my pockets. A car slowed to a stop and a man rolled down the window, leaned out to yell something I didn't understand. I took a step closer to the car as traffic sped effortlessly around him. He repeated what he had said, louder, with a tone of impatience in his voice. Behind me, Walter stood up, yelled something back, not quite angry, but not quite pleasant either. Window still open, the man sped away.

"What was that all about?"

Walter took a socket wrench out of the bag where he'd

thrown his soccer cleats. "He thought you were a hooker."
He knelt down on the other side of the bike.

"He thought I was a what?"

"This street is known for hookers." He stood up again.
"Like this woman, coming toward us." I got a fleeting
glimpse of Sophia Loren gone bad, middle age forced to act
young, a short coat covering a body thwarted by hard use
and drugs. I glanced away.

"She doesn't have anything on under that coat," Walter
said. "Or not much." He got on the bike, started it, nodded
for me to hop on. As we pulled off the curb, we passed
another woman, taller this time, much taller, her short short
skirt revealing square thighs and well-muscled calves, substantial feet squeezed into red stiletto heels. Walter nodded
and she twirled her hand in a coquettish wave.

"Another hooker?" I yelled into his ear, over the roar of
the motor.

"Jesus, Joanna," Walter yelled back, turning his hand to
accelerate around the traffic stopped at the red light. "You
really don't know anything. That one was a man."

I risked my life to look back over my shoulder. I wondered why anyone would willingly choose to wear such
painful shoes.

That night at dinner, Walter put down a set of three pilsner glasses on the table. "Here we are!" The beer was dark red, not quite brown, with a creamy off-white head, a radical change from the Chianti that came in ceramic pitchers, or the green glass bottles of red and white wine. "It's a double malt from Czechoslovakia."

Chad took a long drink and laid his head back along the edge of the bench against the wall. "Holy shit," he said. "I haven't tasted a beer in God knows how long."

"That's a taste that brings back memories, isn't it?" Walter said.

"The Super Bowl," Chad answered. "Best beer ever is during the Super Bowl."

"Listen," Walter said, "I was thinking. Would either of you be interested in a trip somewhere?"

Money was something I never discussed with them, not because I was ashamed, but because they rarely let me. "I have something like twelve dollars in the bank to last me until the first of the month," I said.

"Doesn't matter." Walter said, lapsing into a British accent, rich with entitlement. "Money is no object."

Chad didn't even think about it. "Sure, I'm in."

"Jo?"

"Don't you guys have class?"

Walter shrugged. Chad answered, "I can take one day.

Friday, not Monday. I have a discussion group in the afternoon I have to be here for."

"Where did you have in mind?" I asked.

"Where would you like?" Walter picked up a coffee spoon, turned it over and over in his fingers. "If Chad has three days, it needs to be relatively close."

"Rome," I said, without thinking. There was a Bernini statue there, of Saint Teresa in ecstasy. "Let's go to Rome."

✳

Walter briefed us on his master plan while we were on the train heading south. He said the guards at the Vatican museum wouldn't allow us to lie on the floor to look at the ceiling of the Sistine Chapel. They wouldn't even allow tourists to lie on the benches that line the walls. The chapel was always filled with hundreds of people, gawking at the frescoes. Ostensibly, the Vatican didn't want anyone to be squashed, but Walter said that was a load of bullshit. In reality, they didn't want tourists there at all.

Walter had no intention of being denied his moment with the masterwork of Western civilization. We left our *pensione* at seven o'clock in the morning to make it to the Vatican museum well before opening. Chad grumbled, but the threat of being left behind altogether finally got him out of bed.

We arrived at the museum at seven-thirty for a nine-o'clock opening, but already there was a line. A busload of nuns milled around the entrance, dressed in traditional black

100

habits, with long skirts and long sleeves, heavy rosaries on their belts and in their hands. I listened to them chatter as Walter and Chad backtracked to find an open bar, espresso and some freshly baked rolls. The women were old, their faces soft with age. But their voices were high-pitched and young, skittish as a flock of sparrows. I smiled at the women and they smiled back, touching my sleeve, my hair, my shoulder, like foreign godmothers, a host of guardian angels.

By eight-thirty the line stretched beyond the fortifications and around the corner, out of sight. Exactly at nine, we paid our money. Walter pushed through the crush of nuns congregating just inside the doors, trying to decide which way to go, pulling Chad and me with him. Walter walked quickly past the room of ancient maps, through the hall of priceless tapestries, dodging around statues and vases and elaborate displays of curios. Chad and I had no choice but to follow.

By the time we had gotten through half the museum, we had outpaced the guards, who left the front desk at opening time to reach their proper positions. Walter broke into a run. I laughed, but there was something compelling about the sight of his back, hurtling through the corridors. Chad and I began to run after him. There was no one to stop us. It felt like the freedom of being let out of the classroom on the very last day of school.

When we reached the Sistine Chapel, it was empty, silent like the tomb Mary Magdalene approached looking for Christ. Breathing heavily, sweating under the weight of our coats, the three of us stepped across the threshold and into a place where the air smelled of a thousand spices brought over the Silk Road from China. Dust motes danced in the light from the windows.

I turned once, twice, to take in the scope of the room, the reality of it. I had never seen anything like those frescoes, had never dreamed anything like them would even be possible. My eye lit on a thousand details, the wide eyes of Eve as she was held by God before her creation, the serpent offering a taste of good and evil.

And then it was as if my rational mind shut down. I couldn't think, I couldn't talk. The room shifted under the muscle in Christ's judgment arm. I lay on the floor underneath God and Adam. God stretched out against a cloud, beard blown back by celestial wind, his hand reaching out to touch man, to touch me. The images crushed me flat into the hard tile floor. Color seeped in through my pores. For what seemed like a very long time, there was no noise but the sound of my own breathing, heavy in my ears.

Someone was there. I felt him, I felt her, I felt it—the presence that had no pronoun, no body, no soul. It was the flat surface of the ceiling and at the same time it was us, me and my friends, even though we were small and didn't deserve to be included. God was there and genius was there and we were there. We all fit together in the pattern of creation.

Then I heard wind, the sound of the parting of the Red Sea. It pulled me up onto my feet to face the Last Judgment, a solid wall of human feeling, sorrow, fear, despair. There were no barriers between me and it, no fence, no guards, no bullet-proof glass. The fresco itself started high up on the wall, but even if I could have reached it, I would not have touched. It would have been an act so blasphemous that my hands would have burst into flame.

I saw Jesus raising his hand to cast down the damned. Mary turned her face aside, unable to watch the devils laughing, the men crying. Saint Catherine held the wheel on which she was martyred. Saint Bartholomew held his own flayed skin. The gates of hell opened just above my head.

I could feel the coming thunderclap that would echo through the heavens and the earth. The trees would shake before Christ, the mountains crumble, the creatures flee. In the end, when the angry, the spiteful, and the unforgiving were obliterated, the saints would raise their faces once again and find a world transformed, a world without darkness, one without end.

Then I heard footsteps in the hall. Abruptly, the wind stopped, the feelings passed. I fought the urge to run, to hide. When the first guard arrived, he made Chad and Walter stand. He grumbled a warning so stern that Chad looked away. I thought for a moment the guard might tell me I didn't belong there, that there were places more suitable for me, institutions for the insane.

When the crowds dribbled in, first three, then ten, then hundreds, I began to come to my senses. The three of us stayed as long as we could, walking among the crowd. As the volume in the room rose, the guards turned on a taped message. Silence please, it said, in four or five languages, one after the other. No one paid much attention. Chatter and laughter died down, but not for long. And people kept coming, until we could no longer find room to stand.

Back outside, back in the sunlight, on the sidewalk we'd stood on when we were in line, I blinked against the modern world. Walter admitted he'd had to fight to keep from crying. Chad swore he'd heard music in his head.

✳

At the Villa Borghese, a group of elderly men played bocce. Without exception, their faces were lined, bellies plump, hair gray. But their postures remained important with the work they used to do—banking, perhaps, or some sort of industry. And it was evident from the bellicose way they insulted each other that they still thought of themselves as handsome.

"What are they doing?" Walter asked. We were sitting three to a bench, eating flat sandwiches of fresh mozzarella, tomatoes, basil. Around us, bushes had been manicured to resemble sculpture, and the bark of the madrona trees shone a burnt sienna.

"It's a game, kind of like horseshoes," Chad said. "My father played. Every Sunday after church. Whichever team has their ball closest to the orange target ball at the end wins. You can throw yours either to try to get close or to knock out the other team's ball."

I held our guidebook in my lap, using it as a stiff surface on which to write postcards. I leaned down, close, writing so tiny that the letters looked like hieroglyphs. I told Jack half-truths, that I was in Rome, but not who I was with. I kept silent about my new friends, a pathetic form of revenge for his disregard of me. I planned to flaunt them someday, to drop their names in conversation to prove to him I was not completely without my secrets.

"They'll go blind trying to read that," Chad said, finishing the last bite of his sandwich.

I didn't bother to mention that Jack had perfect eyesight, that I wasn't one hundred percent sure he would bother to read it anyway. I drew a careful line around the address, so I could write even more in the margins.

Chad stood up. "Come here Walter, I'll show you how it's done."

"No thanks. I'll leave it to you."

Chad smoothed both hands through his hair, a mock preparation for battle.

He insinuated himself little by little. At first, hands in his pockets, Chad stood at the side of the field. Within fifteen minutes, he was standing in the group, asking advice he didn't need—pleading ignorance because he was a foreigner. He knew just what to say, and within a half-hour one of the men who had been most gracious was red-faced and screaming, calling Chad a little sack of shit because of his last throw, a toss that had just won his team everything.

"Ciccio. How can you say those things about our guest?" The man who had invited Chad to play in the first place, the captain of the winning team, put an arm around his shoulder. "And such a nice boy. Such a handsome boy."

Chad smiled. "Next time," he said slyly, "the American will go easier on you."

His teammates whooped in appreciation, and even Ciccio, who made a motion to cuff him on the back of his head, had to laugh.

"Can you imagine?" Walter whispered to me.

"Imagine what?"

"He's like the prodigal son. The way those men crowd around him—as if he's one of them. Next thing you know, he'll be invited home for Sunday dinner. They'll offer him their virgin daughters as tribute."

"Bit of an exaggeration," I said, but with his dark hair and Italian clothes, Chad moved with an ease that neither Walter nor I possessed. It was something to be jealous of—he could always, at a bare minimum, pretend to belong. At the same time, it was impossible to dislike him for it, to think he was a phony, to say he was a fake. Just because he was a chameleon didn't necessarily mean he was insincere.

Chad glanced over at the two of us. The way he looked in the afternoon light was like something out of a Tiffany window, brightly colored and ethereal. He waved with a single, triumphant hand, and with a clear, clean grin. Something in the middle of my body seemed to burst.

✳

Thanks to Walter's extravagance, the three of us split a tasteful suite in a three-star hotel across the piazza from the Pantheon. A sign in the room asked us politely, in four European languages, not to throw things out the window.

That night, Walter carried three small tumblers and a bottle of wine into my room. Chad was already there, stretched out on my bed, slightly drunk from dinner.

After the Vatican and a heavy dinner, even I was exhausted. I sat on the floor, my cheek resting against the nubbly weave of the bedspread. Chad ran his fingers over the top of my head, tipsy tugs and tangles that didn't quite hurt, but weren't quite soothing either.

Walter, who had settled in across the room, began to go off, something about Ronald Reagan, a comment Chad couldn't let by unanswered. I closed my eyes and listened to the tenor of their words, not the meaning, the hypnotic tone of male voices matching the disconcertingly subtle touch of Chad's fingers through my hair. I tried to think of something other than him. I wasn't very successful.

Chad crossed the line between a manageable altered state and sheer drunkenness at around ten. He ended up standing on the bed with one fist in the air, shouting something about worldwide revolution, a workers' rebellion that would seize capital from the money lenders. He quoted de Tocqueville on democracy and began to sing "Guantanamera" in Spanish.

"Show-off," Walter muttered.

Chad stepped off the bed, steadying himself with one heavy hand against the wall. He slid down to the floor, wrapped his arms around me, kissed me sloppily in the ear.

"Don't get your hopes up," Walter warned. "He flirts with everyone."

"I do not. I love Jo. Deeply. Passionately."

I slapped his hands away as they began to dig up underneath my shirt. "You do not."

"I do too."

"Well then, you love everyone deeply and passionately."

"Only women." He nuzzled my neck. "And maybe Walter." Across the room Walter raised his glass in a mock toast. Chad's voice dropped to a bedroom whisper. "But I'd rather spend the night with you."

His breath felt warm on my skin. I felt flush, disconcerted, aware of the smallest details about him—the curve of his dark eyebrows, the strength in his hands. I elbowed him in the side. He was only going so far because he'd been drinking, because Walter was there to make it all seem innocent. "Get off me."

Chad settled back against the wall and called for more wine. He halfheartedly reached up to the end table to retrieve his glass. I escaped onto the bed he had abandoned and held the pillow in front of me as cover.

Walter didn't make a move to pass the bottle. "That is the last thing you need."

"Do the walls seem to be moving to you?" Chad asked, eyelids drooping.

"Only to you."

"I do love you guys."

"We love you too," I said, smiling, leaning over to touch him on the shoulder. It didn't take long for him to close his eyes, to slump slowly until he lay flat on the floor.

I looked at Walter. We both sat there, almost laughing, me on the bed, above Chad, him across the room, full ashtray on his lap.

Walter said, "I never knew he had such a love for workers' rights."

I peered over the edge of the mattress. I wanted to put a pillow under Chad's head, to take off his shoes and his sweater, to cover him with a blanket. "His father was a communist from way back."

"Doesn't mean he ever took care of Chad."

"Maybe he did the best he could."

"Who can tell with parents? They're all fucking neurotic."

He didn't realize, saying that, how lucky he was. I would've taken a neurotic parent over a dead one any day.

"So it must get old," he said.

"What?"

"The undying love and attention. The repeated professions of sheer adoration." He nodded his head in Chad's direction. "You must get stuff like that all the time."

"Now I could use another drink." I rolled off the bed and crawled over, on my hands and knees, squeezed in between Walter and the radiator. "So far, Walter, in this life, I have remained strangely undiscovered."

"That's because men are stupid."

We were so close, our shoulders touching, squeezed together in an intimate space. If there was a moment when it occurred to me that I should touch Walter, really touch him, that night in Rome might have been it. Chad had stirred up feelings, a tingling in my stomach, a longing in my hands. In the darkness with the wine, those feelings could've easily been transferred.

But it was clear that Walter wasn't thinking the same thing. I'm not sure how I knew that so exactly. But even drunk, I did.

Chad snorted a bit, his head resting in the crook of his arm. The air in the room changed, as if it were a living thing, took on weight. The longer I looked at Chad, the more unguarded my expression became, until I felt the smile fall off my face. "He's really something, isn't he?"

Walter didn't answer for a very long time. He didn't move, didn't clear his throat. He just sat, staring straight ahead, whether at Chad or at the wall, I wasn't quite sure, until he finally opened his mouth. By then, his words tumbled out into wine-colored silence, and their tenderness glowed warm and three-dimensional in the middle of the room.

"He sure is, Joanna. He sure is."

Our heavy heads touching, Walter and I leaned on each other against that wall. We stared at the object of our mutual desire until we both fell asleep.

SEVEN

*T*here is a painting by Degas that looks as if it is pastel, like a film of chalk that has been smeared by careless fingers, but it is oil on rough canvas that shows through in the white of the dresses, giving them texture and weave. The three women in the painting, who all wear the same dress and are blessed with the same straight auburn hair, have been bathing. The ground underneath is a neutral brown, but there are trees in the background, the suggestion of a riverbank. One woman's shoulders are bare. The back of another's neck is exposed. They seem to invite long, slow, hot kisses, a set of hands and lips to encircle them from behind. I wonder whether I'm the only one who recognizes the man who is not in the painting at all, the man whose presence is everywhere in the way they bend.

W̶hen Jack and I were eleven—the year he got his black felt cowboy hat and I went everywhere in my denim overalls—we found the skull of a cat. It started with a race, Jack tearing after me through the woods after I'd knocked his hat off. We both knew he was faster than me, but I fought dirty, choosing my moments carefully. I'd waited until he was swinging on the pasture gate, then tipped that hat over into the grass. He scrambled to get it and I took off, up into the brush where I hoped to hide.

I saw the white gleam of bone first, stopped short. Jack came up a minute later, panting, grabbing the back of my overalls before realizing what I was looking at.

"Cool," he said. We knelt together to look closer. The cat's skull lay in a hollow at the base of a tree, where the roots splayed to form a kind of pocket.

"I bet it crawled here because it was sheltered."

He nodded. "I heard they're like elephants. They like to be alone when they die."

The flesh had long since decayed or been consumed by other creatures. The bone had no smell and was perfectly preserved. Jack poked a stick into one of its eye sockets, lifted the skull so that we could examine the cavities and the sharpness of the teeth.

That afternoon and for some days later, we hunted for the rest of the body. Jack wanted to find the claws and I looked for movable joints, but they were nowhere to be seen. Under one bush, we found disconnected vertebrae, so small that they must have come from the tail. They had withered, like sticks, to a dry brown color, but we prized them anyway.

Jack let me have the skull. He took the vertebrae and threaded them onto fishing line. He wore them around the brim of his hat, which I kept knocking off until the day Jack lost his temper and jumped on me. Frank had to pull us apart. I don't remember swinging at Jack after Frank grabbed me, but both of them swore that I did.

$$*$$

I hear the crunch of tires in the driveway. I figure it's one of the Rileys—no one else has come out to the farm since I've been back. Still, I'm working over the bench when I hear the sound, so it's no effort to carry my hammer out with me, just in case.

I find Chuck standing in one of the stalls, his hands on one of the sides, probing the bottom with the toe of his boot. He's looking for rot, for breaks, for problems. There are none.

"What's going on, Chuck?"

"Don't you ever answer your goddamned phone?"

I'd heard it ring a couple of times, but it is easy for me to ignore. "I'd rather have people come visit."

"Bullshit."

"You want some coffee?"

"Sure. A little. Too much keeps me up."

I make a motion with the hammer. "Come with me, said the spider to the fly."

"Isn't that follow me?"

"Whatever."

We walk into the workshop. "Holy shit," Chuck says. He's taller than me and brushes his head on my mobiles, the pine branches hanging from the ceiling. He moves to avoid the brown and white bones dangling from the wood. They're tied on with pink and red twine, twisting silently in the wake of his passing.

Tacked onto the walls are huge sheets of paper, painted red and orange and brown, like bricks, backdrops for feather and twigs and not-yet-dry moss the color of new ferns and baby grass. On each one, I've drawn architectural models, like Brunelleschi's cross sections of cathedral domes. The worktable is covered with the lids from canning jars, hammered flat to the size of my palm and to the thickness of a fingernail. In the artificial light, they pass for pirate's treasure, a strange kind of gold doubloon. I have stacked my trophies in crates in the back: the roll of Lifesavers and collection envelopes from the Catholic Church.

"Holy shit," Chuck says again. I'm used to that kind of reaction. Jack is the only one who has always known how strange I am at heart, and he is also the only one who has relished it.

"How long did all of this take?"

Instead of answering, I pull a mug off the shelf, give it a

fast swipe with a paper towel, and pour him some coffee. Chuck already thinks I'm crazy—he doesn't need to know that sometimes I think he's right. Instead I ask, "What's going on?"

"Here's the deal: Rene has a cousin in Spokane who's looking for a cheap place to winter two horses."

Chuck takes a sip of coffee and makes a bitter face. I hand him the box of sugar cubes. "Thanks. They basically plan to take the horses up to the lake in the summer and don't want to be bothered much until then. I thought since your fences were up, maybe you'd want to take them."

"How much are they offering?"

He names a figure that seems high to me, considering that I've already got a pasture full of grass and any number of places to get cheap oats. "Chuck, I know you still have that lot behind the house. Why don't you take them?"

Hands in his back pockets, rocking ever so slightly back on his heels, Chuck out-and-out lies. "Too much work."

"Mr. Riley."

He shrugs. "I got the station. Rene's got the café. I thought maybe you needed the cash."

I look at the gruff man in front of me. "Does this mean you've finally forgiven me for pretending to be Anne Marie Thewliss and sending you those love notes in junior high?"

"Hell no," Chuck says.

"You're too nice to me." I do need the money, maybe more than he realizes, but I can't help but think about my track record of taking without giving. For the first and probably only time, Chuck makes me think of Walter and his extravagance. I look Chuck squarely in the face and wonder how long it might be before he realizes I am selfish at heart and not worthy of his care.

"Everyone deserves a break once in a while." He picks up one of the canning lids, turning it over idly. "So, rumor has it that Jack's coming home for Christmas."

"Really?"

"Talked to his mom. I guess he hasn't come home for years. Since about the time you went away."

"Subtle."

"Seriously. He usually flies his mother over to Seattle, puts her up in a hotel. But this year he's planning on driving out, staying a couple of weeks."

"Maybe he's got extra vacation."

Chuck grins. "Maybe."

"Maybe he just wants a break."

"Maybe he's coming here to see you."

"Chuck."

"Just a thought." He ducks his head on the way out, hits a heavy crossbeam with the flat of his hand. It makes a solid sound that lingers, long after he has pulled away.

The contractors have finished my new roof. That means it is safe to move the sofa in, to put the books up on the shelf. There will be no more stains, no more drips, no more mold. I polish the wood using a thick piece of old towel and lemon-scented oil. The shelves soak up the moisture, drinking it in.

Frank owned boxes of coffee-table books, expensive ones, thick with black-and-white photographs of ranches and logging. There are also biographies and histories, a catalog of parish families dating back to 1888. There is one McGuffey reader that belonged to Frank's father, a small volume with a thick navy cover and old-fashioned script. The binding threatens to crumble in my hand. I find stories that I read growing up, the Velveteen Rabbit and Laura Ingalls Wilder.

Neither one of us was ever much for poetry, which is why it surprises me to pull out a volume of Elizabeth Barrett Browning's *Sonnets from the Portuguese* from the bottom of a box. There is no name on the inside front cover, no indication to whom it belongs, no dedication. I wonder whether Frank borrowed it from somewhere and never returned it, but I don't remember seeing him reading it, don't recall seeing it on our shelves. The other books seem so familiar. Even if I never pulled them down to look at them, their bindings had created a visual pattern that has stayed with me all these years.

I don't recognize the book of poetry, though. Tucked in the middle of the volume I find a note, a tiny off-white card that looks almost as if it has been written in condolence. "Good-bye," it says, a single word. There is no signature, but I don't need one. Since doing the research in the library, I recognize the handwriting as easily as I would recognize my own. It belongs to Hazel Potts.

✳

It can be explained, I'm sure. Hazel Potts worked for Frank and she took care of me. She had every right to give him a book, even if it was a book of love poetry. And there's no proof that she gave it to him in the first place. The note could be nothing more than a coincidence, a marker casually placed in a book.

But it is like a pea has been put under my mattress. No matter where I try to sit, I cannot rest. I try to read and have to get up. I tend to my houseplants and spill water all over the floor. I go to the barn to check on doors that I know have been shut, gates that I remember having already locked.

Before I even realize I have the keys in my hand, I have started up the truck. I knock on Mrs. Stanley's door. She invites me into the house, but I deliberately stay put, out on the porch. I am afraid of being sidetracked by small talk.

I tell her in a firm voice that I need access to the library. Later, I'm sure I will have to apologize, but right now my only thought is that some part of Frank may be buried somewhere in the basement of that building. I have to dig him out.

The library is dark. My hands shake as I punch in the code to disarm the security system. I turn on light after light on my way toward the basement. I don't need the lights to see, exactly—I need illumination. I would set a bonfire if I could, summoning the dead to dance with me.

Some people think that death is the end, but I see Frank every day on the farm, in the stakes he drove into the ground, marking water lines and other places where it was unsafe to dig. He lives on in the truck, the way he made his knots, the elaborate system he used to tie pillows onto the pine seats. I thought I had grown used to the signs. I never expected to see any more.

I leave the library just as dawn is breaking. I have gone through every single box that Hazel Potts left, through every folder and each envelope, searching for what it was that she really meant me to have. I carry out one shoe box full of photographs, full to bursting and held shut with thick rubber bands. On the way home, I drop the keys into Cherry Stanley's mailbox. I won't be needing to go to the library anymore.

✳

The honk of a horn drags me from sleep. It isn't early, but the events of last night have drained me of my will to work. I pull on my bathrobe and open the door. A shiny blue truck sits in the drive. There are three people in the cab, a man, a woman, and a girl in between. Attached to the back of the truck is a silver horse trailer. The woman gets out to check on the horses while the girl comes up the stairs of the porch to talk with me. She is wearing overalls and cowboy boots and has her straight brown hair pulled into a ponytail. On canvas, she would look like a Pre-Raphaelite angel on the tail end of childhood, those last beautiful moments before running headlong into puberty and awkwardness.

"Mrs. Shepherd? We're the Lawrences."

I see the flick of an auburn tail out the open back of the trailer. The girl's voice is swallowed by a sudden memory of the horses I owned at her age. Sheik, who was gentle, older, dependable for me to ride at a young age. The stallion, Blaze, was part Arabian, taller and bold. By the time I was this girl's age, I could saddle him all by myself, take him out onto the road, where fewer things might spook him.

I remember standing in the tack room in the barn, trying to convince Jack to ride with me. Somehow he could always talk me into things I didn't want to do. It seldom worked in reverse.

"I just don't want to," Jack said. He was wearing tennis shoes, shorts, a tank top that showed how dark his skin really was. His hair stuck up in back—he hadn't combed it after waking up.

I was holding Sheik's bridle. The metal pieces knocked together, the sound of tin and wind chimes.

"It'll be fun."

Jack turned from me with a resentful look on his face, as if I were yelling at him for something. "I can call my mom. She'll come and get me."

"You don't know how to ride, do you?"

"Shut up."

"What kind of Indian doesn't know how to ride a horse?" I asked.

"The kind of Indian who had his horses taken away by white people like you."

I looked to see if he could possibly be serious and he did hold his bitter pose for a while, his back toward me, his scowl ferocious, but then I started to laugh and so did he and that's when we took Sheik out and led him onto the road in front of the house.

The Lawrence girl falters because I haven't answered her and don't seem likely to. Her mother calls out in a sweet voice, "Chuck Riley said you could make arrangements for us?"

I look at the girl and tell her I will have to throw on some clothes. She giggles, as if I have said something incredibly daring, and bounds down the stairs. I wonder what she will be like in a couple of years, when the weight of puberty hits her full-force and she begins to like boys more than her horses.

The Lawrences leave behind two animals named Samson and Delilah. I turn the lights on in the workshop and tell the horses I will be working with some drawings. Samson snorts, a living sound in this mausoleum of mine, and I suddenly realize just how long it has been since I have been responsible for the care of animals. Frank was still walking when we got rid of the cattle. He handed over the gate keys to the neighbors instead of rounding up the Herefords himself. When the truck rattled by, carrying the six of them, he was asleep on the couch.

Delilah is an Appaloosa–quarter horse mix and the smaller of the two, with dark speckles scattered across her hindquarters. Samson is taller, wider at the shoulders, and roan-colored, with a reddish coat and mane. I am careful to keep a hand on them when I pass behind so they know where I am, but neither one seems particularly nervous or easily spooked. They nuzzle down into the pockets of my jacket to see whether there are treats buried there. I will have to plant apple slices for them to find.

My last night in America, Jack picked me up and we drove down to the river. He had come as soon as he heard about Frank, taken me to stay up the road with his mother so I wouldn't be alone. We left his car at the dead end where the gravel road ran into the railroad bridge.

The night, I remember, was clear and warm. Jack had left his jacket slung over a kitchen chair. He sailed in Seattle, he said, and I imagined his hands pulling the line to raise the jib. He had a sailor's forearms, muscled and wiry with a thin layer of dark hair.

"When do you have to be back?" I asked. He had just started his junior year and had already missed four days of class.

"Monday," he said. "Do you want to sit or to walk?"

It made no difference to me, I just didn't want to be the one to make the decisions. I'd been making them for days, choices about readings and flowers and food for the reception. I'd made the phone calls to the neighbors, separated the condolence cards from the donations to the church in memory of Frank Shepherd. I was so exhausted I hurt down to my bones.

"You choose," I said.

Jack took me by the hand and we crossed the bridge into the woods where the pine trees did their best to filter out the light from the yellow moon. We talked some, but not about Frank, not about the fact I was leaving. Jack held my hand. At one point, he stepped off the path to pick up a white feather. He handed it to me, with all the seriousness of a man handing a girl a rose. I took it that way.

On our way back over the bridge, an hour later, my legs prickling from overexertion, Jack paused, put his hands on the railing, and looked down at the dark water. The ripples sparkled golden green where they caught the moonlight.

"You want to jump?" Jack asked with a grin on his face.

"Sure," I said and pretended to start over the railing.

"They tore out the ladder, you know."

He was talking about a ladder we had used all the time, nailed directly into the bridge; one that led to the concrete piling below. A thirteen-year-old had fallen when the tie he'd been holding on to pulled loose, rotted clean through. He'd cracked his skull on the cement below, reduced to the mental capacity of a first-grader. It could've been us and we both knew it.

Jack looked at his watch. "What time does your plane leave?"

"I have to be at the airport at noon."

"We should probably be getting back."

But I didn't want to say good-bye. It had been hard enough when he'd left Bright River, hard enough when I could still see him four times a year, when we could talk anytime on the phone. "I don't want to go."

"It'll be good for you."

"It's ridiculous."

Jack put one foot up on the lower railing, his hand on the small of my back. His body heat radiated through my thin shirt. I felt it in my breasts, my belly.

"You've gotten as far as you can go here."

I didn't answer that, but we both knew it was true.

"You would've left years ago if it hadn't been for Frank."

"Maybe I could just move to Seattle. I could stay with you and maybe do some work there."

Staring out at the water, Jack shook his head. He dropped his voice a notch. "You're just scared."

As he said it, we wrapped our arms around each other so tightly that we almost lost our balance. I think he kissed me first, or I may have kissed him. It happened so quickly and was mixed so thoroughly with the years of fantasies I'd had about him, about admitting how I felt, how completely I loved him, that I'm still not sure. I tried to feel the whole length of him all at once, his chest down to his hips, the flesh and the bone, everything. He ran his hands through my hair and down my back, and broke the distance long enough to brush his hands across my breasts, quickly, as if the plane were already on the runway and there were only minutes left, seconds.

Then he pulled away. Or maybe I did. We just stared at each other. My tickets were bought, paid for. He was going back to school. We didn't kiss again.

✳

In a corner booth of the diner, three farmers are finishing their meal. It is obvious from the way they are speaking to each other that they have been meeting here for lunch for the past fifteen years, maybe longer. I look at them to see whether they may be related to Hazel, whether they can answer questions for me. Someone in this community must know something. It is a matter of whether I want to look.

The men are red-faced and heavyset, wearing overalls and baseball hats over white hair. One smokes. Another cleans up the remains of what looked like a burger and fries. When they call for a refill, they don't call the waitress by her name. They call her Sugar instead. She looks about fourteen years old, but must be out of high school or else she wouldn't be working this shift at lunch. The girl wrinkles her nose at them, pretending to be annoyed. This makes the men cackle.

I take a seat at the counter, pulling a menu from its stand by the napkin holder.

"You still like toasted cheese?" Rene's back is to me. She is concentrating on the grill.

I thought I didn't care about food, that I wanted to talk, to ask Rene for her advice. But all of a sudden, a warm sandwich sounds like the answer to all my problems. "With potato chips?"

"You got it." Rene flips two burger patties onto two buns and puts the plates out on the counter for the waitress. Her face is shiny with sweat. "Heard you've been exhibiting some strange behavior."

"Mrs. Stanley?"

"I think you really scared her."

"I think I might have scared myself."

Rene laughs, holds a flat spatula down heavy on the bread. This will create a golden crust on both sides, the cheese squashed and soft in the middle.

"I've missed this place," I say, watching how easily Rene moves between one thing and the next. She steps aside just as the waitress brushes by to fill a pitcher of water, nods at another customer, who leaves five dollars down by the register.

"Nothing like it in New York?"

"Maybe." I think of the Polish diner near my old apartment, the taste of kielbasa and French toast made with thick sweet bread. "But not quite."

"I bet Chuck that I know why you were in such a hurry to get into the library."

I look up, but she is intent on my lunch. I struggle to keep my voice even. "Why's that?"

"Jack told us about your show in New York."

It is not the answer I had expected. It is, in fact, so far from what I thought she would say that it takes me a moment to sort out her words. Jack told her. My show. Another lifetime ago, I sent Jack a postcard, a close-up of one of my charcoal drawings. It isn't true that I had forgotten all about it, just managed to put it behind me, like the memory of a fire that obliterates your house.

"My show?"

"I figure Hazel Potts had something that you wanted to throw into a piece for it."

"My show isn't coming up."

"But Jack said . . ."

"No, it's already over. Just ended, as a matter of fact."

Rene sets my plate in front of me and sits down, drinking soda from an enormous plastic cup.

"You mean to tell me after all that time it took you to actually get a show, you moved while it was going on?"

"Two days before it opened."

"So how did it go?"

I chew on a piece of parsley. "I haven't kept up with it."

"And no one's told you?"

"They don't have the phone number."

"Did you sell anything?"

"I told you, I don't know."

"Do they even know where you moved to?"

I pick up my sandwich and regard it carefully, as if there is a right way and a wrong way to eat it. Do I start with the edges or the points where it has been cut?

"You mean you could have money coming and you didn't let anybody know where you were? How are you going to get your pieces back? How are you going to get a paycheck?"

She looks at me as if I have completely broken through the boundaries of rational behavior. I have heard it before, from people who know a lot more about the art world than she does. Rene thinks my behavior is strange. The flat reality is that it's professional suicide.

EIGHT

✳

✳

✳

✳

Walter brought a red-velvet couch to the studio. He paid two artists the equivalent of twenty bucks apiece to carry it up the three flights of stairs. They were sweating by the end, hard of breath, but good-natured. One, a big-boned blond man from Prague, laughingly called Walter my patron.

"I wish I had one so generous," Tomas said, on his way out the door. "I am down on the second floor if you want to pay money again."

"He's right," I said to Walter. "This really is too much."

He waved away my concern. "As long as you're happy."

I set up my easel and bought turpentine and linseed oil. Lena gave me two old sheets, one for the floor, another to be ripped up for rags. In the trash behind the villa, I found broken panes of glass. I smuggled them upstairs, irrationally concerned that someone might mind, that someone might take them away from me. I could already see a spread of color across them, the rocket flare of alizarin crimson, the stars and stripes bright of cadmium blue.

I stored such treasures in boxes along the wall where I could see them from the sofa, reach them easily from my desk, wine bottles and postage stamps, steel wires thrown into the gutters by the street-sweeping trucks. I collected glass and stamps, not because they were romantic or picturesque, but because I couldn't stand to see them go into the garbage, not when I would look at my cash allowance for the month and choose between art supplies or bus fare, art supplies or lunch.

As for Walter, he took to stopping by at all hours. There was, ostensibly, a guard at the front door who was supposed to protect the art, but he and Walter soon bonded over a few tips, and that was the end of my privacy. It soon became obvious that Walter bought the couch not for me, but for himself, to sit on while he took his shoes off, read the paper, drank his tea.

I balked, at first, having him there. He pretended not to stare, of course. He'd go so far as to unfold his newspaper across the cardboard boxes that served as a coffee table and read headlines to me. But I could feel his eyes on my back when I turned around to mix colors or put pencils away. It was the kind of stare that, in the movies, comes from vampires who gaze at naked flesh, hearing the overpowering beat of the heart.

✳

In late October, I sat at a table at the *osteria,* staring at the owner's youngest daughter. Big-boned like Pino, her doughy face showed every emotion. In the past hour, watching her move through the bar, I learned that she adored her father, flirted with the cook, and disliked wiping down the tables after customers left. In the Middle Ages she might've been shuttled off to a convent, an easy economic solution in the event that no one wanted to marry her. I drew her with candles in the background, a rope of thorns, a cloister arch.

Chad, sitting across the table from me, ran down the index of one of his books, looking for something. He turned to the page indicated, skimmed the entry, picked up a three-by-five-inch card, copied a quote. When he was finished, he put the card in a pile by his elbow.

The *osteria* was fairly quiet at that hour, late in the afternoon, in the lull just after siesta, just before dinner. Pino agreed to let us sit as long as we wanted, with the understanding that we would leave when paying customers came in. We would've left then anyway, because silence was what Chad and I both wanted. Two tables away, a man drank a glass of wine, reading his newspaper. Other than that, we were alone.

Chad tapped his hand on the table, obviously frustrated at something he'd found. He ripped two cards in half, put them aside, got halfway through writing another, then put that aside too. "Can I ask you something?"

I didn't answer. It had always been hard for me to draw and talk at the same time. He went ahead anyway. "What do you think about when you're working?"

I didn't look at him. I set about erasing a series of lines. "I don't know."

"Really."

I paused then, shaking my fingers because the muscles in my hands had cramped. "Nothing, I guess. Maybe about getting it right. Or physical things—whether my hand hurts. But a lot of it is a fog, I just do it."

"That must be nice. Not thinking."

I leaned back in my chair. "When it works it's nice. When I screw up it's a lot of wasted time. At least when you sit down, you learn things."

"Ideally." He let that statement sit for a minute. "I'm working on this debate. It's half my grade in International Systems."

"And?"

"And I found out yesterday who I'm up against. This guy named Mike Mondello."

"And?"

Chad pinched the bridge of his nose as if his eyes hurt. "He was a couple of years ahead of me at Georgetown. Smarter than shit. Used to work on Wall Street."

"You can't honestly be worried about how you'll do."

"You don't know what it's like."

That was true. I'd never had to stand in front of a class and argue a case, never had to take notes on index cards, never had to worry about how my grade might affect my chances of getting hired. But he'd never heard voices, never seen visions, never been mute. I'd lived with the dark circles, the insomnia, the anxiety. I'd made temporary peace with my demons. His were barely waking up.

"Why don't you take some time off? Play for a while. Before your head explodes."

"Play?" He looked at me for a long moment before understanding. "Oh. Cello?" He shook his head. "There's too much work to do."

I laid a hand over his. "You'll be fine," I said, but I shouldn't have touched him. I shouldn't have muddied the moment that way. With the electric warmth of his skin underneath my fingers, suddenly it wasn't about him anymore, not about sympathy or support.

Deftly, Chad turned his hand over, grasped mine. I could feel the touch of his palm, the pressure of his fingers. It threw me back to a moment when I had been held by Jack, when I was so sure that I wanted only him, that I would want only him for the rest of my life.

"Do you realize," Chad said, "that this is the first time we've been alone together since we met?"

The sound of his voice gave me room to escape. I took

it, grateful for the reprieve. "I'm surprised Walter hasn't shown up yet."

At the sound of Walter's name, Chad shook his head. I pulled my hand away, plucked an index card from one of his piles. "So," I said, reading the heading, "tell me everything you know about the political unification of Germany."

"You don't have to do this."

I tapped the card on the table. "Pay special attention to the Franco-Prussian War."

Chad cleared his throat, took a sip of wine, and calmly began to speak about borders and political elites, cabbages and kings.

*

The next morning, I found Walter waiting outside my studio. He walked in behind me as if it were an apartment we shared, no invitation offered, no invitation required. I tried to ignore him, laying out a yellow pad on my desk, Lena's book of saints, my hardback dictionary. I turned to the entry on Bernadette and began deciphering the story of her apparitions at Lourdes. I had marked the pages in the dictionary with sticky tabs, words that came up often, like *blessing* and *holy*, the vocabulary of the beatified, the language of miracles.

Behind me, Walter put down his briefcase, cleared his throat. I could hear the click as he opened the case, the click as he closed it again. He didn't remove anything. Rather than study, he wanted to sit in my studio, to demand my attention bit by grudging bit, until my resistance collapsed, until he got it all.

He hummed, under his breath, just loud enough to be noticed. I gripped my pencil tightly and tried to ignore him, but he persisted in puttering, moving this, straightening that, until even the subtle smell of his cologne began to get on my nerves.

I put my pencil down, searching around on my desk for something to occupy him. I pulled an X-acto knife out of my drawer. "Come over here."

"What?"

I took a piece of scratch paper out of the stack on my desk. "You take a piece of paper. You fold it like this." I made sharp accordion folds with a fingernail. "Then when you cut it, it makes designs. There's wood over in the corner. Use that for a cutting surface. Don't hurt yourself."

"I haven't made snowflakes since I was five."

"You don't have to make snowflakes. Just try it."

"I'm not artistic."

"There's no such thing."

"Oh yes there is. I flunked construction paper in third grade."

"Fine. There's a newspaper on that chair. It's a couple of days old, but have at it. I just need you to be quiet."

I turned away from him then, went back to my reading. It took concentration to come out with coherent sentences. I wrote down what facts I could on my yellow pad.

Teresa of Avila, born 1515. Catherine of Sienna, suffered the wounds of the Lord.

I'm not sure how much time passed before I heard a shuffle at my elbow. Walter didn't say anything, just handed me the sheet of paper with a series of blocked cutouts, abrupt squares, and wide-open spaces. I looked back at the couch, the table, and saw scraps all over the floor.

"What do you think?" he asked, and in that moment he reminded me of a child, someone unused to kindness without strings attached.

"I like it." I pointed with my drawing pencil. "Especially that part there. It kind of looks like a face."

"I thought it was a frog."

"Yeah, I see that too."

"But I did cut that edge off there. I didn't mean to, but I didn't quite have the hang of it."

"That's okay. You can fix it on the next one."

"You think?"

"Sure. If you want. There's plenty of paper."

"Okay." He dutifully leafed through the pile, looking for another color. I turned back to my own work and smiled.

*

When Walter left, I sorted through sketches of women—the women in the market, the women in the street, Pino's daughter, Lena dozing in the living room. I cut certain pages out of my sketchbook with a blade, so cleanly it would be hard later to tell that anything was missing. I laid them out on the floor in a grid, a black-and-white charcoal-smeared game board, three high and eight across. One was a woman who pulled coffee behind the long silver bar in a café underneath Lena's apartment. She wore her hair up in a bun, pinned underneath a ridiculous uniform cap. Her teeth were crooked, stained brown from coffee and cigarettes. She was looking down at the cups with concern.

I drew one of her customers in profile, like the Renaissance portraits of the Medici. She had a narrow nose and dark brown eyes, a pointed chin, delicate bone structure, bad skin. She stared straight in front of her as if she could see past the hills, over the mountains, all the way to the sea.

I sat on the sofa, cross-legged, staring, my hands wrapped around a teacup, as if it held the answers for me. Gradually, as the sunlight coming through the window moved and lengthened, I picked out one of them, then another, a third, a fourth, a fifth. Stringing a heavy piece of twine the length of my studio, I used paper clips to hold the portraits up. The rest I shoved into a folder and left, under the window, with the books about saints I had marked with notes in the margins. The Virgin Mary had planted a seed and it was beginning to break the surface of the dirt. The women begged to be painted, begged in the way they moved with the draft running through the studio, the way they erased the rest of the world from my mind.

On the street outside the political-science institute, I thought I heard chickens. The street itself was quiet, all autumn shades of brown and orange and red, no blue except for the sky, no green left on the elm trees. The morning had been windy and the last of the leaves had fallen under the onslaught, leaving a clear, cold, cloudless afternoon. I checked my watch—five o'clock.

Chad was inside, debating. He didn't want me to watch—not even in the back of the auditorium—so I sat outside instead, on a bench across from the park. The rest of the block was made up of university buildings, arched doorways leading to a maze of courtyards. I looked for the chickens, up in the trees, over in the park, under parked cars. They sounded as if they were nesting, contented and warm. I imagined eggs and white plastic barrels of corn, feed that back on the farm I would've scattered on the ground just outside the barn, so they could scratch and peck. Try as I might, I couldn't find them.

A city bus came to a stop at the corner. The doors opened to let passengers out. A boy came down the steps first, slim-hipped and self-assured. He stuck his tongue out at me and he had a look in his eye, the same one Jack did when we were thirteen, when we were swimming and he stared at my chest. My heart beat in response, as if I were back there, standing in prickling heat, afraid of what my body had become.

Then women swarmed off the bus and around me, a hundred women of different shapes and sizes. They were teenagers and old women, different versions of myself, with red hair and all kinds of body types, every one of the women disapproving, each one of them afraid. They tugged at my hair and opened my bag, they slipped gnarled hands into the pockets of my coat. They wanted to know what I thought I was doing, waiting for a man who was educated and accomplished and normal. They reminded me I hadn't gone to college, that my mother couldn't cope, couldn't even stand up straight most of the time. They told me to look around, to realize where I was, lost in a foreign country and in way over my head.

"Have you been here the whole time?"

Chad's voice pulled me back to reality. I blinked and the women disappeared, the little boy vanished in midair. It took a moment to focus, to bring myself back from wherever it was I had been. "You must be freezing," he said.

I looked at him. Chad was wearing debate attire, a dark wool coat, a wide red power tie. Underneath, I knew he had on a white shirt, khaki pants with a sharp, just-ironed crease. His wing tips gleamed.

I stood up and put my hands in my pockets so he could not see them shake. Other students milled around, chatting in groups of twos and threes. The men had short hair, the women were dressed in black and suede. They all looked rational. They all looked smart.

"How did it go?" I finally managed to ask.

"Very well, I think." Chad struggled to keep a straight face, to maintain some sort of professional composure, but then the posture broke and he smiled wide. "He wasn't prepared."

"I told you."

Chad smiled, touched the side of my face. Then he pulled me into him, leaving no more room for doubt. The different women inside of me squealed, but when Chad kissed me, I couldn't help but kiss him back. I deserved it, I told them, and I was firm in that. I hadn't realized, until I felt the heat of his mouth, how long I had been cold.

＊

"Of course," Walter said the next afternoon. "Of course you heard chickens." He sat perched on the sofa, over a copy of the *New York Times*.

"I thought I was losing it."

"Political science is across from agriculture and animal husbandry. Behind that big wall on the other side of the street? That's where they have the animal barns.

"So you and Chad went out last night?" Walter was good at that, changing the subject, shifting the ground out from underneath me before I realized it.

"Just some dinner." I didn't tell him it had been at Chad's house, that we had sat talking until the candles burned out.

"I was free last night."

"You were?" I sharpened a pencil over the garbage can. "I assumed you'd be busy."

"No more than usual."

Walter picked up one of my books off the floor. *Miracles of Mary*, he read out loud in English, even though the text was in Italian. He leafed through it, the stories of New Jersey and New Orleans, Mexico and Santa Fe. If he'd wanted to change the subject, he could not have found a better way. Just seeing that book in his hands made me feel as if he were peeling back the skin on my forehead to poke inside my skull. I grabbed it from him, placed it on my windowsill with my dictionary and all my notes.

"I wanted to copy the cover art," I said, even though he hadn't even asked.

"Oh. So anyway, you should've called. We could've cleared up this chicken mystery."

"Next time," I said.

He dropped his eyes. "Next time," he confirmed, turning a page of his newspaper. I had seen him whispering in the halls with Paolo, private conversations that he turned away from as soon as he heard my steps in the stairwell. Walter kept things from me. I kept things from him. What made it somehow worse was that now we both seemed to know it.

Rose of Lima rubbed her face with pepper and her hands with lime so her beauty wouldn't tempt anyone to sin. Margaret of Cortona prayed instead of sleeping, subsisted on bread, water, and raw vegetables. St. Colette was struck blind for three days when she ignored the word of God, then struck dumb for three days more. In light of them, it didn't seem too radical to shut and lock the door to my studio.

I set up a mirror by my easel and stared for a very long time at my own reflection, until it dissolved into impressionistic dots. I rocked back and forth in my chair.

The first week, I tried to capture their eyes. Mixing cadmium blue with linseed oil and turpentine, I diluted the color with titanium white and a raw umber, earth and flowers, egg yolk and metal. The woman in the coffee bar became Catherine of Sienna, who subsisted on the Eucharist while brokering peace between medieval popes. Pino's daughter turned into Bernadette, poor and illiterate in a way that was not noble—vaguely squalid and embarrassing instead.

The second week, I drew their faces close-up and wild, half out of focus. I surrounded their heads with halos, gold rings, and layers of metallic dots. Weed green leaves crept over their chins, tigers and monkeys leapt somewhere in the background. I drew crosses behind them, then covered those crosses up. They were there, but invisible, the symbols of suffering, the promises of salvation. I experimented with everything I could think of, with trees and rosary beads, clerical robes and flowers. I discarded them all in favor of sunken cheeks and pale pink skin, ascetic features but healthy color, an inner strength and the fury of judgment, the hint—somewhere in the middle of the prayers about peace—of eternal hell.

I used all the canvases I had, painting on all five of them at once, layering in the background colors, adding elements over the top in waves. I built up and out, putting on colors and scraping them away, until each one became an almost three-dimensional piece made of invisible brush strokes and an infinite layer of paint. They saw right through me, these women, the way that I painted them, they knew it all.

I was swept away by their spirit and their unattractiveness, their pulling away from the world, their pulling away from men. Theirs was not an ordinary life. Those women perpetuated the ecstasy of mystical vision, they drew it out until it was a single thread, stretching to the horizon, connecting them to expanses of sky.

*

At the end of each night, I couldn't leave them alone. I went out only to eat, when I remembered to, a fatty sandwich one day, a bag full of tangerines the next. They were Amazons and queens and holy women, and I couldn't lock them away behind a plain door in an ordinary square room, sharing their secrets with each other instead of me. For three weeks I slept there, on the red velvet-couch, huddled under two wool blankets. I dreamed of medieval cities. I painted in my pajamas. I forgot to comb my hair. And it was like flying, with no engine and no parachute and a fear of falling that couldn't keep pace with the thrill of being up in clear skies, blinded by the sun.

I don't know when my mother crept in. I don't know how she put her face into the canvas, how she guided my hand to sculpt her eyes. It seems crazy to say I didn't recognize her, didn't understand quite what I was doing until she was already there. In my mind, Teresa of Avila was supposed to look like a nun in the marketplace who still wore a habit, the nun in the marketplace who smiled with gentle reflection on a little girl. Instead, she was young and scared and confused, doubtful that she was worthy of much of anything, certainly not the faith God had put in her. She was Teresa, who would become a doctor of the church, revered the world over because of her clear confessions of her mystical union with God. She was my mother in a private moment of doubt, unsure whether she would be able to bring forth a life that was unwanted. I had been waiting for a sign for so long that I had stopped looking. Then, when I least expected it, that sign appeared.

From time to time, Walter knocked on my door. I didn't let him in. Once, just once in that period, I dialed Chad's number. He wasn't home.

*

Weeks after shutting myself in with my paintings, I reemerged. It happened unexpectedly, with very little forethought. I had planned on going to Lena's to sleep, but every time I closed my eyes, I could see only colors, the frost white blue of a winter sky, the liquid gold of paint. The smell of turpentine filled my nostrils, stuck to my hair.

I stood at the edge of their table at the *osteria* for an instant before they broke their conversation and looked up.

"My God. If it isn't the prodigal daughter," Walter said, looking vaguely startled.

"Walter."

My voice sounded strange, and I realized I hadn't spoken to anyone in a very long time. The conversations I had been having inside my own head had echoed so loudly that at times I worried I'd been shouting.

"You look awful," Chad said, standing up to take my coat and scarf.

"Thanks."

I hadn't changed clothes for a few days. When everything I owned got paint on it, it didn't seem to matter.

"You've lost some weight."

"Really?" And that was the first it occurred to me I'd forgotten to eat that day, for the most part of that week. I could feel my skin from the inside out, shrinking.

As I slid in next to Chad, Walter motioned to our waiter. "Let me get you a drink."

I hadn't realized how overwhelming it would be to talk to them again. They didn't know what was back at the studio, who was there, watching, listening, praying in the moonlight. I didn't want to tell them.

Chad draped a hand across the back of the bench. I leaned back into his arm and felt the tips of his fingers brush my shoulder. I think I had known, even before I walked down the stairs into the bar, that I wasn't looking for dinner or wine or even their company. I was looking for him.

Walter cleared his throat. "So how's the work going?"

There was a pack of cigarettes lying open in the middle of the table. "Can I have one?"

The men exchanged a look. They both knew I didn't smoke. "Sure," Walter said, handing me the pack.

Chad lit it for me, his left hand, the lighter, and his face close to mine. He dropped his other arm, cupping it deliberately around my shoulder, cradling me. I wondered whether I had the resolve to act sane when all I wanted to do was run my fingers up through the roots of his hair and pull him into me. Painting had opened doors inside of me, shutters of emotion.

I swallowed hard. "So, you guys were in a hot-and-heavy conversation when I walked in. Let me guess, Chad was explaining the CIA overthrow of Salvador Allende in Chile."

Walter stabbed the air with his cigarette, relieved, I think, to see the moment pass. "Close! Actually, Chad was describing *Three Days of the Condor*."

"I still can't believe you've never seen it. Classic. Robert Redford. Lauren Bacall."

"Actually," I said, not quite trusting my voice, "I think it was Faye Dunaway."

"Once again," Walter said, "Joanna brings a tone of reality to the conversation."

Before my eyes, they seemed to shift back into the men I knew. But sitting there by Chad was too much, I couldn't control anymore what I thought, what I felt. I wanted to forget about Jack altogether, to wipe away the pain of losing Frank. I wanted Walter to need me less or not at all. I wanted Chad's weight to smother me.

＊

Walter called first thing the next morning. He caught me at Lena's before I left for the studio. "So! Are you really back for the long haul or are you going to disappear again?"

"I wouldn't have called it disappearing."

"Do you want to meet for dinner later?"

I'd already made a date with Chad on the way out of the *osteria*, a whispered aside while Walter was paying the check. I wasn't about to share. "Actually, I think I'll probably be working late."

He didn't answer. In that silence, I could feel what the separation must have cost him, the fact I had cut him off from his comfortable world on the edge of my couch. I twisted the telephone cord around my finger, anxious to be off. "There must be a lot of details you need to think about," he finally said.

"In a way."

"Can I see them?"

"See what?"

"The paintings."

"I don't feel comfortable showing them right now."

"Not even to me?"

I remembered standing together in the Vatican, staring at Michelangelo's *Pietà*. Chad had gotten tired and Walter and I stood there for minutes on end, staring at the curved surfaces, the flow of Christ's arm, as if Mary might look up, as if her son might come alive. The two of us breathed in seeming unison. I remembered feeling Walter's hand on my shoulder, turning me away, the only thing making it possible to separate from such a polished statement of grief. If it hadn't been for him, I would be immobile, still standing there.

I did owe him a great deal, and even though I didn't fully want to, I made an offer. "You could come by this afternoon."

"Actually, I'm busy this afternoon."

"Tomorrow?"

"Really tonight is better for me."

But at that moment, Chad was more important to me. Looking back, that would've been the time to tell Walter what was going on, to warn him that relationships were changing. Instead of explaining, I simply said I couldn't. I was as intransigent as he'd been, and in my own way as dishonest.

✳

At the political-science institute, they converted the cavernous front hall into a disco by moving out furniture, hanging white Christmas lights. Chad paid the money at the door and pulled me through the dance floor, past men groping and women breathing heavily.

"Walter's not going to be here, is he?" I yelled, scanning the crowd.

"God no. He hates anything that has to do with school."

We ended up in a storage room that served as a coat check. There, in the dark, pressed up again other people's tweed, Chad pulled out a bottle of Jägermeister from the inside pocket of his coat and took two quick drinks. I couldn't refuse when he passed the bottle. I was still trying to get over the medicinal burn when he kissed me hard, twice. I wanted to eat his tongue, to open my mouth so wide the kisses wouldn't stop. He fumbled with my shirt, pulling it up at the waistband of my jeans, slipped both hands around to the small of my back.

When other students came in with their coats, we moved out to the main room, where I drank enough wine to forget the fact that I didn't know anyone. Chad and I danced together as if we were alone in a house where no one was ever coming back. His breath felt hot against my neck.

For once, I wasn't lonely or awkward or wondering. I wasn't stranded or waiting or having a conversation by myself. The only time I took my arms from around him, I reached into the air. With the raising of my arms came an elastic expansion of my rib cage, the soft tissue between each bone inflating with every breath like a warm pink balloon.

By midnight, the crowd had grown appreciably larger. Someone turned up the music, we had to yell to be heard. Even on the edges of the dance floor, we were pressed together, endangered by flying arms. Standing in the middle of all that made me light-headed, the mix of Jägermeister and wine leaving me sick.

"I have to go," I whispered, not because I wanted so badly to be alone with him, but because the heat and the noise were too much. I dropped Chad's hand and fought my way through the crowd, from the warm into the cold, from the womb into the world.

Outside the institute, the street was quiet, frosted, dark. Heavy doors and stone walls muffled the music, but it rang in my ears, even in that open space. I took one deep breath, two, and stared at the empty neighborhood, the pools of yellow light thrown down by the streetlamps.

When Chad opened the door behind me, the noise of the party spilled out over the sidewalk. I turned my head, looked at him, preoccupied with buttoning his jacket. It was a cloth coat, brown, with a corduroy collar, functional, plain. It looked familiar to me, as if Frank might have owned it. If I had any doubts about him up to that point, that moment erased them.

He glanced up at me. "Are you all right?"

"I just had to get some fresh air."

"Where do you want to go from here?"

I didn't want to drink more. All the coffee bars and restaurants had long since closed. Decent people were all at home in bed. "Are Giovanni and Mauro home?"

He nodded. "Plus Mauro's brother and a friend of his. They're camping in our living room."

"Oh."

"Your house?"

I shook my head. With Lena there, it would be worse than doing it under the nose of a parent.

Chad paused. "Can I tell you something?"

"Sure."

He put one hand against my face and looked at me with real sweetness. "You have the most beautiful eyes."

I didn't realize until he said it how long I'd been waiting to hear a sentence like that. My body seemed to soften into him to the point where everything else was inevitable.

"I don't want you to think I'm trying to talk you into bed."

"But you are." And I couldn't help but laugh because it was true and because it didn't matter. "My studio is close."

"Cab close or walking close?"

"How soon do you need to get there?"

Chad laughed at that and put his arm around me.

✳

He cleared my pads and books and papers off the sofa. I lit candles. When I sat down next to him, Chad didn't say a word. He just leaned in to kiss me.

The room was completely silent except for the brush of clothing and our breathing. It seemed to last for a very long time, the kissing, the testing, the tentative tries to reach a little more skin, to touch a more intimate spot.

Then Chad altogether unbuttoned my shirt, slid it off my shoulders, began to remove my bra. All the while, he stared at me. I wondered about the rest of them, the women he had been with, and wondered what they did better than me, whether he expected something I didn't know how to do. I wanted to stop it all, to ask him for help. I wanted him to say something, to tell me how to move my hands.

Instead, he took his own shirt off. He lifted it up and over his head, the way boys do when they're going swimming, all elbows and chest. A dark wave overtook me and I didn't have to ask him anything at all.

After that, there was one more point, a quiet moment, a drawing back, when the breathing seemed to stop and we looked at each other. Chad touched my cheek, my face, with the whole flat of his palm. We were naked by then and I thought maybe we wouldn't actually go through with it, that we might simply hold each other and drift off to sleep.

"Relax," he whispered.

"I don't know how," I may have said. Or I may have just thought it, thought it so strongly that he understood. Chad began to kiss me again, so many times I lost count. My soul seemed to open up to let him in.

He didn't know it was my first time and I didn't want him to know, so when he entered me, in spite of the pain, I pushed up just as hard as he did down.

At least the couch was already red.

NINE

*M*ary Cassatt drew women sitting in front of mirrors, arranging their hair. She puts them center stage at a moment when their thoughts are unguarded, pastel blue and private. She records the textures of their lives, the stripes, the flowers, the pattern on a silk fan. Art historians say she borrowed her style from the Japanese, where such a depiction of women is standard, traditional; but I think it's more than that. I think Mary Cassatt, unmarried and independent and talented, knew that there is no more powerful moment in the day than the split second a woman seriously asks herself, Am I beautiful? Will I ever be?

I take the cover off the box and remove one photograph. There must be dozens of them, all different sizes, most black-and-white. I pick one at random. Frank sits in the saddle, twisting to look at something on the horizon. I can't even see his face, but I know that it is him by his posture, his shoulders, the way he is framed against the sky. He is a cowboy in a baseball hat, a shotgun strapped to his saddle just in case.

The handwriting on the back identifies him and notes the month and the year, six months after my mother left Bright River for Spokane, a year and a half before I was born. I have to blink through tears, and I sit with that photograph the way a mother would sit with a sick child, silently rocking in my chair.

The one on the horse is the first in a series of farm life. They are numbered irregularly, so it is obvious Hazel took pictures of other men and other farms, but kept these aside, bound together in a box for her to look at and for me to find. With gloved hands, touching only the edges, I lay them out carefully. They take up most of the surface of my table. Without exception, the prints are clear, taken from close-up, out in the pastures and the fields back behind the house. She has Frank tilling, planting, harvesting, a man in boots, in jeans and a work shirt.

Hazel Potts has done a masterful job. She captures the grace inherent in Frank's range of motion, in the saddle, on the ground, standing annoyed at a steer who has bolted away. Her photographs are austere. They mark the barrenness of a hillside without natural water, the wind burn on Frank's unshaven cheek. He is younger than I ever knew him, thick across the shoulders before illness melted them away.

✳

The workshop is full, so I move out into the wider barn where unused stalls become shelves for objects and big square beams are the anchor for sheets of paper covered in paint and ink. Indian summer is gone for good. Rains have come, rains that edge toward snow in the ferocity of the winds that accompany them. It is cold in the barn and I lay a tarp down over the dirt so I can leave a space heater safely running. Sometimes I play the radio, sometimes I work in silence. Sometimes I talk to the horses, who confer with each other, then answer. I break to eat sandwiches and to drink coffee, mucking out their stalls in the late afternoons.

My work takes a turn to incorporate hair, which might seem dead to some people, but is alive to me, as alive as bones and teeth and Lifesavers. I borrow it from the horses, unwinding long strands of mane so they don't break halfway through. When Chad combed my hair, he held it at the roots with one hand so I couldn't feel the tug of the brush in the other. I do the same with the horses. I look at the red in

Samson's mane. Holding it up to the light, I realize it's the same color as mine.

✳

Rene mentioned my New York show to Jerry Baker, who digs through his back issues of the *New York Times* to see whether he could find any information on me. He finds the article, complete with photos and a sidebar that chronicled the reactions of minor celebrities. It is strange to see my work small and grainy in black-and-white. I feel myself slipping in between the dots, past the images into the paper itself.

"They say you're missing."

What they don't realize is that it means less to me now than it ever did. I stare at the principal, willing him to leave me alone. "All I can say is that they haven't been looking very hard."

"Rene says you don't know."

"Know what?"

"Your sales figures."

"Not a clue."

He looks at me, smiles, as if he knows this information will make him more attractive, as if I will suddenly fall into his arms for delivering it to me. All I can think of is that he thinks too highly of himself and dresses in suits I do not like.

"Your show sold out."

"Pardon me?"

"Your show. Apparently every piece was purchased."

I look down at my coffee. "Really."

He stares at me as if I am some kind of anthropological exhibit. It is a familiar feeling. Chuck does it every time he mentions Jack.

"It probably wouldn't have done nearly so well if I'd been there for the opening."

"That's not what the article said. You're supposed to be the next Andy Warhol."

"I'm not sure that's a compliment." I try to joke, but blood has suddenly rushed to my head. It occurs to me that I haven't been sleeping well lately. I wonder whether I am making this up. I seize on the fact that the saltshaker on the counter is almost empty. In case of hallucination, I am sure, I would imagine it full. I blink. There is no change in the light, not the way there was when Mary came. The principal waits. So does Rene. They clearly want me to say something else.

"It was a small gallery."

Rene shakes her head. "What does this mean?"

"She's famous." Jerry takes a sip of coffee, then keeps yammering away. "Didn't you know?"

Rene snorts. "Jo's not famous."

This arrogant man is at an advantage: he has read the article, I haven't. To grab it means that I'm interested, to grab it means that I care.

Jerry shakes his head. "If the front page of the *New York Times* arts section isn't famous, what would you call it?"

159

Rene stares at me and I meet her wide eyes. Even though I haven't seen her for years, she can still read me the way she could when we were kids. She recognizes the defeated slant to my shoulders. She wants the truth even more than the principal does, but knows the best way to get it is to take care of me.

"So the question on everyone's lips is why you ran away," the principal says.

"Pie?" Rene asks, insinuating herself between me and the man. "We have Dutch apple, cherry, chocolate cream, sour-cream chocolate cake, and vanilla ice cream. Would you like dessert? You usually have something, don't you?"

Before he can begin to decide, I am out the door, a dollar slapped on the counter to pay for the coffee.

✳

On the phone, Jack doesn't say hello. He doesn't ask how I am. He starts in, as if the distance between Bright River and Seattle, the distance between us, is of no consequence at all.

"Rene called."

"Great."

"She wants to fax me a copy of the article in the paper."

I can hear noise, the ring of another phone and—despite the hour—I know he is calling from work. A voice in the background interrupts, asking about a shipment of ice axes.

Jack covers the mouthpiece before yelling back an answer. I wonder if he has gained weight too, like Chuck and me and Rene, or if he is still so thin that the muscles in his bare arms ripple under the skin. With all of the climbing he has done, I can imagine his legs are strong, ready to carry the world.

"Good. Then you can tell me what it says."

"You really haven't given them your address?"

"It's not like I'm really trying to hide. If I were, I wouldn't have moved back home, for God's sake."

"They must have really pissed you off."

I toy with the plastic phone cord. To tell him the whole truth means going back to the beginning, to Florence, to Chad, to Walter. It means asking whether he really loved Kayla, the woman he used to be engaged to, out in Seattle, the one he lived with while I was in New York. It means asking whether he believes in God or thinks, like everyone else, that I have always been a little crazy and that's the way I will always be.

"They were hanging my work wrong," I mutter instead. It is the truth, just not all of it.

"What?"

"I walked into the gallery and it was all wrong. They were advertising it like I was trying to do this pop-culture religion thing, which isn't what it was about at all. And there was a lot of pressure to include certain pieces I didn't want included." My chest grows tight.

Jack waits. He stops typing, as if he is trying to read the silence on my end of the line. I gather myself enough to say, "I thought it was what I wanted, but it didn't turn out to be like that."

He doesn't ask me to explain. "Are you okay?"

"Yeah," I say, but my voice is small.

"Do you have plans for Christmas?"

In times of stress, I always find it best to resort to sarcasm. "I'm going away with Mom, Dad, and the rest of the kids."

He ignores me. "Spend it with me and my mom. I'm driving over on the twenty-third."

I don't answer him. There are no words for the physical reaction I have to the sound of his voice, the thought of seeing him again.

"Date?" he asks, and for that instant, it is possible to believe I'd never been with Chad at all.

"Date," I say.

"And Jo?" He tacked on, just as I was about to hang up. "Yeah?"

"Let them know where you are."

✳

It is difficult to even look at Hazel's photographs of me. It is clear that I loved and trusted her, or else I wouldn't have sat so still, wouldn't have kept playing while she took shot after shot of me and my stuffed bear. I didn't mug for the camera, giving up a false smile the way children learn to do. Instead, I look vaguely worried or angry, as if my toys were not listening to my commands. The clothes I wore were a little too big.

Sitting in the barn alone and undisturbed, I daydream instead of doing work. I imagine Hazel reading me a story. She sits next to me on the sofa in the living room, my thumb in my mouth, a blanket clutched in my other hand. After kisses and prayers, Frank takes me off to bed. He is in stocking feet because his boots are muddy, out in the garage.

It is painful, this idea, that there was more to this relationship between my grandfather and this woman than one of employment. It makes me wonder why she didn't choose to be my mother. What was so wrong with Frank, what was so wrong with me, that she didn't want to stay? I hear Hazel talking me through my grief for my mother, teaching me to fix images in chemical baths. We stand together in a room bathed in red light. She tells me why she takes so many photographs. Together, she says, we can capture time.

*

I have a half dozen of the pictures of Frank enlarged at a copy shop in Spokane. By the time I make it back home, it is late afternoon, when the shadows have lengthened and the sun blazes a soft gold. It is into that rarefied air that I unroll the posters across the floor of the barn. I put coffee cans full of nails and screws on the corners to keep them flat. These six are my favorites, and I am seized with a kind of fever that comes when the realization

163

of an idea is even brighter and stronger than the idea itself. Rarely has anything felt quite so good as seeing Frank's profile bigger than life. Through tricks of scale, the farm has become a Hollywood backdrop, a stage for an epic descent into madness, an inevitable rise into glory.

✳

Of all things, the newspaper in Spokane sends out a reporter. I don't hear her until she's already in the barn. She must have parked up by the house and walked down. The horses whinny briefly and I hear the sound of the metal cowbell hung in the square open doorway. It is rusting and the sound is chunky, pastoral, out of place.

"Hello," she says, as I come out of my workshop, wiping my hands with a ragged white towel. I have been taking down the scenes of Florence, the architectural sketches based on my memory. I want to hang up Frank instead, the one where he is sitting at the workbench, his face in shadow. The focal point of the photograph is the ax that he is sharpening, sparks flying off the electric wheel in a white phosphorus arc.

"Hello." My breath comes out white. It is cold there, in that open doorway. I'm dressed in my flannel pajamas with long underwear peeking out, Frank's checked logging coat over everything. It's a pleasant surprise to realize it doesn't bother me, to be seen this way, the way I really am.

"I'm Jill Barnes," she says, as if the name alone is supposed to mean something to me. *"Spokesman-Review."* She is easily forty, but trying to hide it with red lipstick and elaborate hair. Her clothes look out of place, shiny synthetic fibers, perfectly pressed. She reminds me of the women in department stores who spray perfume on passersby.

"Jo Shepherd."

She smiles and tilts her head as if what I've said is amusing. Of course she knows who I am. "I've gotten several calls suggesting that we talk to you."

"You have?" I leave her standing in the doorway and walk over to the horses. They snuffle in my outstretched hands, searching for sugar.

Ms. Barnes pulls out a notebook and leafs through it, as if she doesn't already know exactly what she's doing. It's a self-conscious gesture, stolen from television. "One Jerry Baker and a Chuck Riley."

The principal I might have expected. I will have to kill Chuck, though. I pull some hard cubes of sugar out of my inside jacket pocket. I keep them there, wrapped in plastic.

"We'd like to see whether there's a story here."

The horses nuzzle up the treat with warm lips and still want more. "Will you be wanting pictures?"

"Kip's in the car." She answers, smiling, as if I know who Kip is, as if she's had an amazing amount of forethought to plan for this contingency.

I'm supposed to crave exposure, but I don't. I know about this kind of woman, even though we have never met. She will ask what she considers to be simple questions.

What is your medium? What does your art mean? But they've never been simple to me.

If I'd wanted the attention, I wouldn't have turned my back on New York. I never would've left Manhattan. What I crave right at this moment—aside from some offhand desire for chocolate ice cream—is to get back to rearranging the barn, a therapeutic straightening of materials that will give way for Hazel's work and mine.

"This is a waste of my time," I say. It is abrupt, I think afterward, but she took me by surprise. I don't want to share anything with her, certainly not Frank or Hazel.

"What?"

"I don't want to talk to you." Like a dog responsible for the well-being of sheep, I herd her out, out of the barn, up the drive. I don't touch her, I just walk close and she has no choice but to move.

"Are you sure? It's just a short piece. Maybe if we make an appointment?"

There is a thin man leaning up against the hood of their blue Lincoln Continental. He has a camera around his neck and is staring at the house, as if framing it in his head.

"No."

"That would at least give you time to think about it."

"Good-bye," I say, careful not to add "nice meeting you" out of habit or some misguided attempt to smooth over what I've just done.

Kip, the photographer, sums up the situation at a

glance. Maybe it happens to them often. Maybe he's just astute. "Get in the car, Jill."

When he tells her to do it, she does. As soon as he can turn the car around, they're gone.

＊

Frank's Christmas decorations are packed in random-sized boxes marked ORNAMENTS and X-MAS and simply LIGHTS. I bring them up one by one from the basement on Thanksgiving, while my turkey roasts in the oven. The stuffing is made with garlic, herbs, and butter—I can smell sage roasting in the bottom of the pan.

I plug in the lights, stringing them out in four straight lines across the living room. They glow while I put on my heavy coat, my work gloves, pick up the tin bucket, head out to the shed for some firewood. The hatchet is sharp, its edge gleaming straight and silver, making it easy to split kindling. Back inside, the shavings catch easily, the paper under the wood turning as red as my cheeks, then bursting—under the weight of my breath—into flame.

Instead of listening to the radio, I put on a worn-out record, Tchaikovsky's *Nutcracker Suite*. It is an old recording, from sometime in the fifties. There are dolls on the album cover, white-faced porcelain, dressed in elaborate costumes, an innocent girl in a lacy nightdress, a handsome prince in a red jacket with gold braid and buttons. There are skips in it, scratches I caused a long time ago, jumping around, pretending to float like a ballerina. I expect them, the repeats, the glitches—they are worn like grooves into my mind.

In the kitchen, I busy myself by poking at the turkey, by peeling potatoes, and setting water to boil. Maybe I'm crazy, to rush the holiday this way. But I can't help it. I admit something to myself: I am looking forward to seeing Jack.

✳

Cherry Stanley drives out to drop off a package for me. I am embarrassed to see her after the way I demanded her keys. Part of me feels small, called to the carpet for something I already know was wrong. She stands on the porch with her coat collar pulled up to her chin, obviously cold, just as obviously unwilling to step into the kitchen where it is warm. I offer her coffee. She does not even bother to decline. She just holds out a box for me.

"This is your property, Joanna. I thought you should see it."

"Where did it come from?"

"Another UPS shipment came in. They'd apparently lost a few boxes. This one has an old label. With Frank's return address on it."

"Thanks."

She looks at me. "You left so much material for the library."

She is talking about that night. She must have expected me to haul away the entire collection. But there would have been no reason for me to keep more than Hazel really meant me to have. "You can take much better care of it than I can."

She smiles, softening a little. "I thought that you might hold a grudge."

"Because of Chip?"

"He never did like you," she says.

"No, he didn't."

"He said you brutalized him, you and your friend Pearce."

"Chippie made fun of the fact that my mother wrapped her car around a tree. And he called Jack names because his father was Indian."

Her hand tightens around her collar. "Chip was ten years old," she says.

"And he got what he deserved."

She changes the subject abruptly. "We'll be sending you paperwork to make the donation official."

I nod and she gets in her car and drives away.

✳

Inside the box sit letters, pages in envelopes, and little notes folded into squares. I don't take them out at first. I just look at the paper, a sheet or two of pink or yellow, some different colors, but mostly white. I run a finger over the ragged edges, where sheets have been torn from a pad. I want to know and yet I don't.

I take a handful of notes out of the box, unfolding the first, then the second, then the third, stacking them in the order in which I pull them from the box, as if that is of some kind of mystical importance. I breathe slowly and quietly as if I have just started a marathon.

I offer myself bribes. An ice cream sundae if I don't run away, enough whipped cream and nuts and chocolate to feed a family of four. A shiny new circular saw. A trip to Spokane just to eat Thai food, noodles in black bean sauce. When my hands start to shake, I snap the rubber band I've put around my wrist.

"Is it absence or abstinence that makes the heart grow fonder?" Hazel's note is torn from a pad like the ones Frank used to keep by the phone. I wonder whether he was asleep when she wrote it, whether the yellowing piece of tape at the top stuck it to the refrigerator. "I'm not satisfied with either option."

I unfold piece after piece of paper, take letter after letter out of the box. I find thin invoices for film and a receipt for paint—the kind that I used on the walls of the barn when I was little. Hazel had ordered it over the phone, her name written in on top by the clerk.

There is almost nothing with Frank's handwriting on it, no measure of sentiment for her in return for the jokes and the news and the declarations of love. It is a heavy burden, her correspondence, and he seems to have disappeared under the weight of it, perhaps embarrassed by the words she was committing to paper.

I hope, for her sake, that his affection was shown in other ways. He might've chosen to be practical in his expression, building a new darkroom in her studio or buying flowers that she liked for the beds in front of the house. Or he might have been more like me, unable to express it at all, except too little, often too late.

"Do you really love me?"

This note was written quickly, in handwriting that is so large and so unlike Hazel's normal hand that she was clearly distraught. I find it after one that says, "I will call you from the hospital," which must have been immediately after Elmer's heart attack—Elmer who may or may not have ever known that his wife was having an affair.

Do you really love me? In Hazel's question, I hear an echo of my own pleas to Chad, to Jack, to the rest of the world. I search through the pieces of paper, but do not find an answer.

*

The weather has turned bitter for the winter, the ground is white with permanent frost, the sky clear and glittering cold. Delilah tosses her head as I pull the cinch down, bloats up her stomach so I have to repeat the action a couple of times. The boots I wear for riding pinch my feet, penance for my years-long abandonment of them. I ride with a wool cap pulled over my ears and a scarf wrapped around my face. My breath, misty and warm, catches in it.

We walk together, the horse and I, through gate after gate. I lean over to open, maneuver her through. Each time, the leather in the saddle creaks, as if it is old and strained and tired. Delilah, once she realizes she cannot brush me off by walking too close to a fence post, settles down into a slow and steady rhythm, the back and forth of a rocking chair.

"Good girl," I finally say, leaning forward to pat her on the neck. Then I clamp down with my knees, kick at her sides with my heels. She is a child's horse, unused to exercise. She needs to be persuaded. I kick her again and yell.

She trots at first, an awkward jolting movement that makes my teeth hit together a few times before I relax, before I remember how to use my legs. She moves from a trot to a canter, a canter to a gallop. When the mare hits her stride, I lean low over the saddle to catch less wind. In my imagination, I am an Indian and a cowboy both and there are no other people in the world. There are only trees in the distance and the stark black foothills of the mountains. I am in control of the direction I take.

I ride until my fingers cramp and my legs hurt and I am cold, deep down in the center of my chest.

I spend an afternoon with Chuck and Rene because Rene insists. Chuck sits in front of the television, sunk into the couch, yelling at the Dallas Cowboys. He surfaces during the commercials, but only to get another beer. After so much time in relative silence, the television unnerves me. It is like a jolt of electricity applied directly to the brain.

Rene sweeps me out into the garage to see her brand-new freezer, which is avocado green. Rene has had it only a week and when she throws open the lid it is already full, of frozen pizzas and anonymous packages wrapped in white butcher paper stamped with blue.

"Chuck went out hunting a while back. That's part of the reason we got the thing. Plus the kids. You know."

It is strange, the way she wants me to like her new appliance, as if it is a wild animal she's just tamed. I smile and do my duty, asking about cubic feet.

The Rileys' house is warm and comfortable, with a day-in-and-day-out kind of child grime. There are plastic toys in the entryway, liquid soap in a Winnie-the-Pooh dispenser by the sink. The Rileys' youngest is one year old and waddles through the house in diapers, his hands trailing over upholstery and walls. He reaches up for plants, but Rene has set them tantalizingly out of reach. "He likes to eat dirt," she says. "We've already had him dewormed twice."

"You've got to be kidding."

"Don't even get me started talking about the older ones and lice."

It is in the kitchen, while Rene puts the scalloped potatoes in the oven and sets me to chopping the tomatoes for the salad, that I tell her about Hazel. She stops what she is doing, slips the oven mitt from her hand. While I am talking, she takes two beers out of the refrigerator. She opens both of them and hands one to me. I explain about the photographs, about the letters, how I imagine they met, how I imagine they broke apart.

When I am finished, Rene has a half smile on her face. "Frank Shepherd. Who would have thought?"

"She really seemed to love him."

"But she also went with her husband to Arizona. You don't know that he didn't love her too. I mean, you only have one side of the story. Not even that."

I think of the possibility of having grown up with a mother and can't help saying that I wish Frank could've found a way to make it work.

Rene takes a long drink of beer. "You don't know what happened. Why are you so quick to make him the bad guy?"

I don't want to tell Rene that it is because I am afraid, afraid that my inability to communicate is hereditary and that it will cost me every intimate relationship that I may ever have. It is not the fact that Frank had a lover that disturbs me; it is the fact that he lost her, the fact that we both did. It is like finding an alcoholic in the family tree.

I don't want to tell Rene, so I shrug instead, trying to fight back tears. The beer only seems to be making it worse, so I set the bottle aside.

"Besides, it's obvious that he cared deeply for her."

"Why do you say that?"

Rene stares at me with the kind of look that she might give a child who is acting stupid on purpose. "In the box, whose letters are they?"

"Hazel's."

"Not Frank's?"

"No. That's my point."

"That means he kept them, Jo. He kept every piece of paper she ever wrote on. Or close to it. Then he made sure she got them before he died. He had to go around, find her address, do it behind your back so you wouldn't find out. He packed them, addressed them, and mailed them to her. What does that say?"

I shrug.

"Don't get defensive with me. Just think about it."

I imagine Frank keeping the scraps of paper close to him, in the bottom drawer of his desk, maybe, or in the top drawer of his dresser with his watches and cloth handker-chiefs. I can see his square fingers, folding and unfolding notes like origami, the way he squinted when he read fine print.

"It means," she goes on for me, "that he wanted it resolved in some way before he died. I don't think you can assume that because she didn't keep his letters that there weren't any. Maybe your grandfather was doing the best he could." Rene throws her bottle in the trash. "And maybe that has to be good enough for you."

"But . . ."

"People aren't perfect. Not your grandfather. Not Hazel. Not you. So stop agonizing."

I get the distinct impression that we're not just talking about Frank anymore.

Rene walks over to the stairs and calls up to her girls to set the table. They come running down the wooden stairs all at once, rounding the curve at the bottom with a dramatic leap. Rene rolls her eyes at the noise.

"The good tablecloth, Mom?" the oldest one asks. The four-year-old uses two hands to scoop silverware from a drawer.

And that is all we say on the subject of Hazel Potts.

TEN

A few days after the party, Walter asked Chad to go skiing with him, but said he couldn't invite me. He had planned the trip for months, he claimed, Christmas break with three other guys from their program. Chad apologized over the phone, although it was easy to tell he wasn't really sorry.

"There just won't be enough room," he said.

"Don't even lie to me."

"What?" But I could hear the smile in his voice, the feigned innocence.

"Like Walter would ever choose economy accommodations."

"So it's a chalet. But it's a small one."

"When are you going to tell him?"

We had made love twice since the night in the studio, enough to conceive of how it might feel to say "we" instead of "I." But Chad had already made the point that the relationship was in its early stages and that we might want to ease into things one step at a time.

"I'll tell him as soon as we get back," he said in a tone of voice that made my stomach jump. "Don't get into any trouble while I'm gone."

I laughed at the idea, tempting fate.

*

I spent a quiet Christmas Day with Lena, who walked with me to church through lightly falling snow. For dinner, she roasted garlic and fennel and a choice cut of beef. We drank wine and exchanged small gifts.

Lena's daughter called. I watched the old woman laugh and cry, heard her praise me and lament the fact that her family could not be together. After the phone call, Lena insisted that I had to call someone, that there had to be one person in America who wanted a Christmas wish from me. She would pay for it, she said, no matter how long I wanted to talk. I told her she was too extravagant, but she simply wrinkled up her nose.

On a whim, I called Jack at his mother's house in Bright River. My heart beat wildly at the thought that he might answer, but when the phone picked up, it was Mrs. Pearce. I wished her a happy holiday and she said Merry

Christmas in return. The connection was rough, our voices traveling across a cable buried deep under the sea.

"Is he there already?" she asked.

I thought I must have misunderstood. "Who?" A ghostly echo of my own voice came back over the wires.

"I didn't think so," she said, which didn't make sense, but her next sentence came through loud and clear. "He's not even supposed to take off for another half hour."

There was no other *he* for the two of us. "Jack's coming?"

"Did he tell you? He said it was a Christmas present, a surprise."

My left hand began to shake, just a flicker. I put it in my armpit and held it down, as if that would make everything all right, as if I could that easily suppress the effect that Jack had on my body.

"Jack's coming," I repeated, and could only think, hysterically, that Chad was away, that Walter was away, that no one would ever need to know.

"I told him I didn't think it was such a good idea. You could've had all sorts of other plans."

Yes, I almost blurted out, I could've slept with someone else in the meantime. I clamped my teeth shut so that no sound could escape.

"I know from experience, honey," she kept on, "some surprises are just too big."

She wasn't exaggerating. In Seattle, Jack would be stepping cheerfully onto a plane, with no thought that he might end up in quicksand. If he'd asked, I would've warned him against me. I would've told him not to come.

✳

I ran to my studio, down empty streets, past windows filled with white Christmas lights. I slipped once, but did not fall, as if saints and angels were somehow protecting me from my own folly. I ran until cold air filled my lungs, until I gasped against the beauty of the snow.

Fumbling with the key to the villa's side door, I almost gave up, almost circled the building to look for a break in the garden wall. Once in the building, I turned on the hall lights and they flickered in protest, as if they knew it was a holiday and they shouldn't be asked to work. I took the stairs two at a time.

In my studio, I covered the women with white sheets, taped down the corners and folded the edges so that nothing showed. I didn't want the color to leak out, for their feelings to betray me. I checked under the sofa for telltale signs, for a man's sock or a folder I wouldn't be able to explain. I threw away Chad's assignments that I had been using as scratch paper. I didn't want Jack to ask me about them. I didn't want him to care.

When I met Jack at the airport in Milan, he took me in his arms and held me so tightly that my feet left the floor. As tired as he must have been, between the time difference and the hours on the plane, Jack held me up, made me feel as if there was nowhere else I was supposed to be.

He smelled like rain and he felt like home, the rough texture of his flannel shirt familiar against my cheek. The knot in my stomach untied as easily as if it had been made of silk. I could feel the muscles in my shoulders relaxing, my body responding to his.

"Surprise," he whispered.

Then the way he moved his hands reminded me of Chad. I abruptly let go, but we still stood absurdly close, as if at any moment we might touch again.

"You should've told me you were coming," I said.

"Did my mother call you? I thought she might."

"Actually, I called her. I wanted to wish you a Merry Christmas."

"Well." He took a half step back. "Do you think you can stand having me for a week?"

"I guess I'll just have to make do."

Lena put Jack in the room across the hall from mine, served him his morning coffee exactly the way she served it to me. He thought it gracious, but I suspected that Lena, who prayed to virgin saints, wanted to make sure this affable American stayed in his own bed.

＊

On our first day out in the city, Jack and I ran into Tomas, the Czech painter who had become Walter's friend, walking across the Ponte Vecchio. He shook our hands with vigor, eager to share a coffee, anything to postpone work. At the bar, I went to the bathroom and came back to find Jack telling him a story about a BB-gun war Jack and I had fought with Chuck in the woods around Bright River.

I shook my head at Jack. "You are incorrigible."

"He started it. He's read Zane Grey."

"I traded with tourists for copies," Tomas offered. "It was one way to learn English. And now I meet a real-live Indian."

"Half Indian," I corrected, "and what that has to do with shooting at each other, I don't know."

"I never thought to meet even half an Indian," Tomas said.

"Besides," Jack protested, "it's a good story."

"So"—Tomas leaned forward—"you are in the woods. And you see this Chuck with gun walking by."

"Did you tell him it's a BB gun?"

Tomas looked at me. "What's a BB gun?"

"Jack. He thinks we're running around shooting each other with real rifles."

Jack explained the difference, but I could tell Tomas didn't really understand. When he retold the incident back in Prague, we'd be wearing hats and boots, carrying six-shooters on our hips.

Jack told of following Chuck, up behind the barn and to the reservoir where the stream was dammed up for the water supply for the house.

"And he sat down behind a stump and waited. He didn't know I'd been following him, so he thought he'd get above me on the trail and wait for me to come by. I watched. I waited. And when there were footsteps on the trail, Chuck poked his head out. I could just see the blue of his baseball cap. He aimed his rifle . . ."

"His BB gun," I interrupted.

"His BB gun. Then he shot Jo."

Tomas howled. "No!"

"I was just bringing them sandwiches," I said.

"And he shot the bag right out of her hand."

"No, he didn't. He actually shot my hand."

Jack laughed. "That part isn't true."

"It is true," I protested. "And when you tried to shoot off Chuck's baseball hat, you hit him between the eyes, and your guns got taken away for the rest of the summer."

"He didn't shoot your hand."

I showed them the scar, a pink circle just below the second knuckle. "Frank had to take me to the hospital. He took Chuck too. I remember sitting there, waiting to get stitches. Frank bought us candy from the machine and proceeded to tell Chuck what idiots you both were."

"I have a scar from camping experience," Tomas proudly said, rolling up his sleeve. "Trying to heat a can of soup on the fire. I forgot to put holes in the can. There was a big explosion. I am burned from hot beans." And he showed us the wrinkled skin, just above his elbow.

"Mine's the best," Jack bragged and unbuttoned his shirt enough to reveal a line on his chest, just above his heart. I remembered when he came home from summer camp with the bandage. He couldn't go swimming for days, couldn't get the stitches wet.

"At camp, when I was a junior counselor. Willy Strobeck tripped on the archery range and the arrow went straight in."

It was utterly unreal, to catch sight of his skin in such a casual way, in such a public place. I'd wanted to touch the scar all through high school, long after it had healed, and I wanted to touch it now. I wanted to be twelve again, walking up the trail to the reservoir, to hear the trickle of the stream. I fought the urge to run my fingers across Jack's scar, across his collarbone, up toward his mouth.

Jack caught me staring at him and paused in the story just long enough to let me know that he knew what I was thinking. And Tomas looked from me to him and back again, then laughed and laughed and laughed.

✳

After dinner, Jack told me that Rene was going to have a baby. We sat side by side on my bed, the lamp on my desk the only source of light. The full-length mirror on the front of the wardrobe reflected our image back to us. Inside, on the door, were pictures of Jack, fixed to the wood with clear tape. He didn't know that I looked at him every day, a photograph of the two of us on the top of Mount Spokane on a sunny afternoon and one from when we were relatively young, on the backs of our horses in the middle of the field. I wouldn't open the wardrobe to get a sweater out, not while he was there. I wrapped a blanket around my shoulders instead.

He wanted to see some of my art, but there was none there, so I sketched him instead, the way his hand rested on his bent knee. I couldn't have looked at his face and he couldn't have kept still, not when he was describing Chuck's reaction to the news. He was ecstatic, Jack said, and told Rene then and there that they were going to get married.

"They want you to come home for the ceremony."

I smiled. "That would be something else."

"Do you want to?"

I looked up from the drawing, from the charcoal lines on the off-white paper, and was hit with a wave of mourning so strong that I had to lean back, to support myself against the wall. I could feel the confines of the property, the fences of Bright River. I would not be able to set foot in that house without knowing that Frank had died in the front room, without knowing that I had fled. The grass, the posts, the trees would all be tainted with grief.

Even Jack, sitting next to me, darkened, as if a light had gone out. He reminded me too much of my grandfather, from the timbre of his voice to the way he shrugged his shoulders. He had apprenticed himself to Frank and had come away with more than plumbing and home repair.

"It's too soon," I managed to say.

Jack took the pencil out of my hand, closed the sketchbook, and laid it flat on the bed. When he spoke, his words were barely audible. "You're not the only one who misses him, you know."

The ceiling in the room was already low, but it seemed to drop even farther, until it skimmed the tops of our heads and threatened to press the air from my lungs and tears from my eyes.

"Do you know what he did the last time I saw him?"

I shook my head.

"Frank had me drive him to the bank. He wouldn't let me come in with him. And I wanted to. I mean, he could barely make it in with his walker." Jack stared straight ahead, not talking to me as much as remembering for himself. "One of the bank tellers had to come out and open the door for him. But he wouldn't let me help him.

"I wait. It takes him about ten minutes. So he comes out and I drive him back, then help him into the house. We talk some, about nothing in particular. I'm just about to leave, and he hands me an envelope."

Jack's eyes began to water, but he didn't wipe the tears away. He kept staring straight ahead. "He hands me this envelope and says to take it, says it's a tip for everything you've done for me." His voice was rich with the irony of it all, as if we, the children, ever had as much to give Frank as he had given us.

"What was it?"

"A hundred dollars. In new bills." Jack put one hand over his eyes.

I put one hand on his back, but I couldn't feel anything of him through his layers of shirt and sweater. So I reached up to touch the back of his neck, where the skin was warm. He breathed deeply, then turned his head to look at me.

We sat, staring at each other, frozen. I heard the roar of wind past our farm, the kind of gale that sent people to their cellars, knocking heavy pine trees into power lines, showering us with sparks.

Sitting side by side on the bed, our faces were close, our bodies even closer. Jack leaned into me. And at that moment, I didn't have the courage to relax back into the intimacy we had shared on that bridge in Bright River.

Jack thought he knew me, but he didn't. And it felt strange to be sitting there, with him, instead of with Chad, whose body I had come to know. I couldn't pretend that nothing had changed, as if Jack and I were still at home, where the rules were unspoken, yet understood, so when Jack leaned in to kiss me, I turned my face away.

Confusion crossed his face, but only for a moment, because instead of pressing forward, Jack abruptly stood up. He moved over to the window and unlatched it, throwing both sides open to the street. The cold air of winter rushed in.

I watched as Jack climbed up onto the window ledge. He stood there, his feet as wide as the ledge itself, framed by a rectangle of light, spilling in from the streetlamps outside. Two stories up, he grasped the wooden molding on the sides of the window, bracing himself so he could lean far out over the sidewalk. He laughed then, crowed almost, as if he were Peter Pan and he could fly.

"Come down," I whispered, but instead of listening to me, Jack leaned even farther, testing the limits of his own strength. I could see him on the roof with my grandfather, reaching for lemonade. He wouldn't mean to fall, he wouldn't mean to cause his own death, but an accident could still happen. It would only take the slip of a finger, the letting go of one hand, and he would fall away from me.

"Jack!" I said more sharply, then he did come down, for a moment. But he didn't look at me, didn't seem to notice that I was there and that I was terrified. Instead, he scanned the room, looking for something, but before I could figure out what it was, he had already walked over to the desk lamp. He put his hand under his sweater and untwisted the bulb.

"Come here," he said, climbing back up on the windowsill, so I went to lean over, to see what he saw, to take in the quiet night, where frost dusted the gray stones of the houses across the street.

A woman strode by, her hand up to her collar to keep out the wind. Jack waited until she was three steps beyond us, then he dropped the lightbulb onto the street. It fell as if in slow motion, glass down, metal up. The woman took one more step, then the bulb smashed into the cement, shattering into dust, a circle of particles like the crater of a bomb. The woman jumped, as if she had been shot, then looked around, angry.

I ducked my head and Jack jumped down, back into the room. Pushing his hair back out of his eyes, he grinned, as if he had been childishly wicked, like egging someone's house on Halloween.

I felt sorry for the woman on the street. And at the time, I wanted to push Jack out the window for scaring me.

***

"You seem different," he said at the Uffizi, as we stood in front of Leonardo da Vinci's *Annunciation*. I had no answer. I had been trying to keep us too busy to talk, too worn-out to repeat the scene on the bed. We went to museums, we stood freezing at the top of the Duomo. Jack ducked his head entering the monastic cells at San Marco, he followed me into the market to look at the heads of wild boar. I knew from the way that he'd politely allowed me to play tour guide that he didn't understand what was going on. He wondered, without saying it out loud, why I wouldn't let him touch me. I tried to show him how profound the effect of my new environment was, the fact that immersion in a different culture had altered my perspective of myself. Jack nodded when I tried to explain about dimensions in sculpture, apparently not understanding that it had anything to do with him.

***

One morning I got up before first light and went to the studio. As early as it was, I wasn't the only one there. On the ground floor, by the pottery studio, I could hear the showers running. At least one person had spent the night working.

On the second-floor landing, I saw light coming from under Tomas's door. Before I had given it much thought, I knocked gently, poked my head in. He sat on a tall stool, staring at an easel. He must have had a half dozen lamps plugged into various outlets around the room. His room was larger than mine, and warmer because the windows were fully sealed. In addition, his floor actually seemed level. The whole studio was meticulously clean, the floor swept, the garbage placed in a can lined with a plastic bag. On one wall hung an Eastern Orthodox cross. It was the only ornamentation.

"Sorry to bother you," I said.

He shook his head. "I am not sure what to do with her," he said, nodding toward his painting. It was a study in color, the face of a woman of substantial weight but indeterminate age, her hair pulled up into a coarse black bun. She was clearly a woman who worked with her hands, a farmer's wife perhaps. She had wide shoulders, a green throat, almond-shaped purple eyes.

"There is something missing, but I either start all over again or I leave it. I'm not sure."

I would've told him to leave it, that her eyes were too expressionless to be redeemed, that a green throat was too much of a distraction. But Tomas didn't ask for my opinion, so I didn't offer one.

"Do you have any coffee that I can borrow?" I just wanted to sit in my studio, hidden away from Jack.

"I will trade with you."

"I have a bunch of broken glass upstairs. And some canceled stamps from America. You're welcome to any of those."

191

He smiled. "Walter says you have been working on a series."

"True."

"Can I come up sometime? He says it is women saints. I would be very interested."

"No one has seen them yet. I'm not sure I'm ready."

"Whenever it is a good time," Tomas said. He walked over to a counter, picked up a maroon foil package of Illy Caffè. "But I'm surprised. No one has seen it? Not even your American friend?"

"Especially not him."

Tomas handed me the coffee, sat back on his stool. With his long arms and long legs, he looked precariously balanced there. "Doesn't he go back soon?"

"In about three days."

"I do not understand. I was under the impression that you two are . . ."

I shook my head. It was the last thing that I wanted, for a rumor to get back to Walter, through him to Chad. "He's just a friend."

"You do not seem particularly happy about that."

"It's complicated," I said.

Tomas nodded gravely. I could tell by the tilt of his head that he was expecting some kind of explanation.

I blurted out a question instead. "Have you ever painted something so personal that you were afraid to show it to other people?"

"Me? Not really."

"I'm afraid he'll ask too many questions." I didn't know how to talk about the women without talking about my vision, how to talk about passion without mentioning Chad.

"There are things that you don't want him to know?" Tomas asked.

"Pretty much."

Tomas ran two hands through his hair, leaving it sticking up at odd angles. He took a deep breath, let it out again. "I don't know about your friend. But I do know art does not stop when you put down your brush. Your painting, when it is finished, is not an objective thing. It is not a table or a lamp or a bed. It is a bridge between you and the world."

I glanced over at his heavyset woman. Tomas followed my gaze. "My work is not as powerful as yours," he said wistfully. "I have nothing yet to hide."

I blinked, suddenly fighting tears. Quietly, I thanked Tomas and went up to my studio where I sat, not working, staring at my own blank walls until it was time to go home. I left the foil package on my counter, its seal unbroken, the coffee unmade.

*

The morning of his last day, Jack sat at the breakfast table drinking a glass of orange juice. I washed dishes, setting them to dry in the small wire rack next to the sink. He tapped one finger on the table, a sound that was barely perceptible yet insistent at the same time.

"I thought we might take the bus up to Fiesole," I finally said just to fill the silence. "They have Etruscan ruins there and you can see the city."

"I don't want to," Jack said.

Because I was doing the dishes, I couldn't see his face. I tried to ignore the tone in his voice. "You don't have to worry. We'll be back in time for the celebration tonight." It was New Year's Eve and we had planned to spend it in the city center, where there was to be a festival complete with fireworks.

"That's not what I'm worried about."

"It's really pretty up there."

I heard the scrape of his chair, then felt Jack's two hands on my shoulders. They were weighty, not to be argued with. "I want to see your studio."

I shut off the water, tried to avoid him by reaching for a towel to dry my hands. "It isn't that simple."

He pulled me back, into his body. I could feel his breath in my ear. "You have led me around like I am a trained puppy. I don't want to do it anymore. I want to see your work. And you know there isn't any more time."

"I'll give you the keys. And directions. You can go by yourself if you want to that much."

"Stop it," he said, giving me a shake, but it wasn't his voice I heard, it was Frank's.

I twisted away from him. "This is hard for me."

"And I don't understand why."

I opened my mouth, then shut it again. Explaining

wouldn't have been any different than showing him the work. Either way, I would have to admit what I had done.

*

At the studio, Jack squatted on the floor, his body made small so that he could stare at the saints face-to-face. They glowed, their wraps gathered around them on the floor, as if he held a flashlight trained right on them. He didn't ask for explanations. He just listened, to Bernadette with her cow-like eyes and Rose with her pockmarked skin. He moved close, then backed away. I willed him to feel the tropical heat of the jungle, warm sap running through dark green leaves.

Jack leaned forward, followed the curve of Saint Teresa's face with his finger. "There is something about her in particular," he said.

"Teresa of Avila."

"Why is she important?"

"She's one of the doctors of the church. She had mystical visions most of her life. Of Christ mostly, but other things too."

"But why did you paint her?"

With those brief questions, Jack wormed his way into a place where I'd never intended anyone to be. He poked a finger between my ribs, through my skin and tissue, as if I felt no pain. It made me angry, his intrusion, as if he had a right to demand of me anything that he wanted. I would give him the truth. It was no less than he deserved.

"She's my mother."

If I had expected him to be surprised, I was wrong. He didn't seem particularly dismayed that I was working on portraits of my dead mother. He simply looked at her.

Absurdly, I toyed with the idea of introducing them formally. In the normal course of things, they would have long since met. My mother would have fixed him dinner when he was ten, worried about his driving when he hit sixteen. Or she would've kept me in the city altogether and away from the farm. If she hadn't died, I might not have met Jack at all.

He cleared his throat. "You must have been thinking of her since Frank died."

"I guess so."

"And all this time, I thought it was about me."

"What?" I asked, even though I already knew.

"Your preoccupation."

"Have I been preoccupied?"

Jack turned, then, and something in his profile reminded me of Chad, the way he looked when he was studying and I interrupted his train of thought. It was the look of patience, marshaled at some cost, as if Jack were fighting not to be annoyed. "Joanna," he said, with warning in his voice.

"This visit hasn't been what you've expected, has it?"

"I didn't know what to expect."

But I'm pretty sure we both knew that wasn't true. "Certainly more than you've gotten," I said.

"I'm leaving tomorrow. You're just now showing me your painting. And only because I forced you. What you've done is incredible. And I can't believe you kept it from me this whole week. It's not like you."

I saw Chad, then, lying on the couch with his shirt off, reading while I worked on sketches of him. I felt his arms around me and the way his lips tickled the back of my neck. In adolescence, I had dreamed that it would be Jack. Now, I had met someone else, become someone else myself.

"I wish you would've written to me," I finally whispered.

Jack rocked back and forth on his toes, his arms across his chest. "Is that what this is about?"

"I waited and you didn't write to me." The tears welled up in my eyes.

"I didn't do a lot of things last semester." He looked around for a place to sit and finally settled on the very edge of the couch, as if he could not allow himself to be entirely comfortable. "I didn't even go to class half the time. I just couldn't manage, not after Frank died."

That thought hadn't occurred to me, that his grief might be debilitating in a different way from mine. "I thought you might be angry at me," I said.

"Angry about what?"

I swallowed. "The bridge. How it might change things."

197

Jack shook his head, that smile on his face again, the small one, the sad one. "How could I be angry about that?"

Simple, I almost said, you could've been angry if you didn't love me. You could've been angry if you thought I wanted too much from you. I bit my lip instead. "I didn't know what you thought about it, afterward."

He shrugged. "Maybe I did try to stop thinking about it. For a while. It was so overwhelming, the feelings I had for you. About us. The fact that you left. The fact that Frank was gone. And it was all mixed up together. Maybe I did try, for a while, to stop thinking about you. But it didn't last long. Then, when I tried to write, I couldn't even get the words out. I just wanted to see you."

"I wish you could've told me that."

"I'm sorry I didn't," he said. And then there was silence in the room for a long time. I stood there, thinking about what I had done, how I would tell him about it, until he finally asked if I could come and sit next to him on the couch.

I did, as close as I could get. He put his arms around me and I sat there as long as I could, my head against his chest, listening to the beat of his heart. He kissed the top of my head and I let him, let him stroke my hair, until I simply couldn't lie to him anymore.

"I have something to tell you," I said. I started by describing what I had seen in the kitchen back home, using my hands to create the illusion as surely as if it had been in front of me. I told him about the voice and the way I had disappeared into it.

By the time I got to the bridge, the night of the kiss and what it meant to me, I could not keep still. I paced between the windows and the couch, faltering at the point when I tried to tell him that I loved him.

And later, when I was on my knees on the floor in front of him, I couldn't talk at all. Jack had to ask questions, Chad's name, the dates, to pull the words out of my mouth as surely as if he had used his hands.

I could not feel what he was feeling, could only imagine the effect of my words on him. After he finished asking questions, Jack fell silent. He would not meet my eyes. I reached for his hand, to reassure myself that we were still close, but Jack took his hand away. He didn't have it in him anymore, he said, to be the one to comfort me.

∗

By midnight, Tomas, Jack, and I had waded through the crowds into the middle of Piazza Signoria. We stood surrounded by the rest of the city, our eyes on a wooden figure in the middle of the square. Tomas uncorked a bottle of red wine and we passed it freely between us. The seated figure of an old man, a simple effigy of the past year, stood twenty feet high. Carpenters had hammered him together in the square the day after Christmas—he'd been waiting all that time to be set on fire.

As the square filled and people pressed closer, men in medieval costumes piled kindling underneath the figure, bundles of dry sticks tied with string. Someone set off a cherry bomb and the crowd roared, ready for celebration, ready for blood.

At midnight, church bells rang out across the city. One man held a torch aloft, and as the crowd roared he set fire to the figure. It caught quickly, flames licking their way up his legs to his chest. From the top of Palazzo Vecchio came fireworks, white bursts of light that made flowers bloom in the sky.

The orchestra, seated on the steps of the Loggia dei Lanzi, began to play. Speakers on all sides of the square carried the sound of Viennese waltzes, and everyone began to dance. Jack took the hands of a young girl wearing a red felt hat and twirled her in circles, while I was taken by her father and pulled up into an embrace. Tomas tapped a jig by himself, bottle in one hand, the other up in the air. We waltzed in the same square where Savonarola had built his bonfires, where he and his followers had burned books and paintings and other vanities, where he himself had been burnt at the stake. That night, we paid homage to pagans who'd marked the solstice with flickering light. The flames warmed our skin.

It was magical, Jack's last night with me, a celebration

of seasonal change. But we didn't kiss, not even at midnight, when it meant nothing more than holiday cheer. I'd lost faith in my best friend and taken to bed a different partner. It seemed that neither one of us could quite get over my desertion.

ELEVEN

Walter arrived at the *osteria* first. I got there while he was still standing, taking off his coat, settling down at the table. Chad came fifteen minutes later, after the wine had been poured and the pasta ordered. He yelled out to Pino and the women behind the bar, greetings for the new year. For me, he had a full-blown kiss, an intimate touch at the small of my back, exactly as if Walter weren't there, as if he were completely unconcerned about the effect the kiss might have.

Across the table, Walter cleared his throat. "Well," he said. I flushed, unable to meet his gaze.

Chad shrugged off his coat, put his arm around me, and looked straight at Walter. For the first time, I saw Walter at a loss for words. He seemed to shrink in his clothes, as if they were suddenly too big for him. He swallowed his wine quickly, wiping his mouth with the back of his hand. His wit seemed to have utterly failed him.

"So when did this happen?" he asked. He pretended to look at his watch. "Since we've been back from Cervinia for exactly forty-eight hours, I'd say last night is a good bet."

Chad just laughed, as if it were a joke. He took his arm from my shoulder and put it on my thigh. "We thought we'd wait until after the trip to tell you the good news."

"And what good news it is," Walter said sarcastically.

I looked from one to the other. Chad had told me that the trip had gone well, but from the way Walter was acting, it seemed unlikely. There had never been this much tension between them. Something had happened while they were away.

"What is it?" I asked, but I could tell by the expressions on both of their faces that neither one was about to say. They stared at each other, jaws set, eyes determined. Looking from one to the other, I suddenly felt cold.

Then Walter lit a cigarette. With the first drag, he gained some of his composure, some of his color. "I don't suppose the timing of your news is particularly significant," he said, talking to Chad, not to me.

Chad shook his head. "We just thought you should know."

"I assume this affair began before our trip?" Walter asked.

"Does it matter that much?" I asked.

"It does since Chad wanted a free ski trip. And he wanted to make sure nothing fucked it up. He must have figured that if he mentioned beforehand that the two of you were sleeping together, that it might upset me."

"It wasn't anything like that," I said, glancing at Chad. His expression hadn't changed. And all of a sudden I couldn't be sure.

"Walter," Chad warned.

"Am I wrong?" Walter stabbed out his cigarette, looking at Chad. "Or are you just embarrassed because I'm actually saying it in front of her."

"Why are you so worked up?" Chad asked.

Walter threw his hands up in the air. "Worked up is exactly the way you want me to be. Pissed off. Angry. You want to get to me. And you figure this is the easiest way to do it."

Our pasta arrived. Walter ignored the food altogether, pulling on his coat. "I think, for once," he said, "the two of you can manage to pick up a check."

Pino yelled something good-naturedly as Walter stalked out. He didn't receive a reply.

In my studio, the wind tore at the broken windowpane. The cold had reached in with invisible fingers and pushed at the glass until it fell, inward, shattering on the floor. I had hung panels of white material in lieu of curtains, a piece of a lace tablecloth, several strips of threadbare sheet. They danced and billowed in the wind.

"I just don't understand why it upset him so much," I said.

Chad curled up his hands and blew on them. "Do you realize you can see your breath in here?"

"Give me a minute." I began to search through boxes for a roll of duct tape. "I mean, it's crazy. Why would you purposely try to make him mad?"

Chad squatted over the radiator to see if he could coax it to produce more heat. "This isn't working."

"I'll get it."

I strapped a piece of cardboard across the broken window and sealed the edges with the tape. Chad watched while I took a pair of pliers and turned the radiator all the way on. With a hiss, hot water flowed into the pipes.

"You're good at fixing things," he said.

I could tell he was trying to soothe me after what had happened, but it didn't work. "You haven't been listening to me."

He shook his head. "That's not true. I just think that these are all things you need to ask Walter. They're his business."

I laid my hands directly on the radiator and closed my eyes. There was a limit to how much I was willing to pursue it. I simply didn't have the energy. Jack had been gone less than a week. Less than a week, and already I was beginning to wonder whether I had made the right choice. I couldn't get over the feeling that I had traded Jack for Chad—Chad who couldn't fix a window, Chad who didn't even know how to use a pair of pliers.

And then Chad came up from behind, put his arms around my waist, began to kiss the back of my neck. I tried to pull away, but he wouldn't let me go. His kisses grew longer, as he leaned more heavily into me. I braced myself against the radiator, then against the wall. I turned to put my arms around him. Chad slipped his hands up under my shirt and wiped away my reservations.

✳

The following morning, I couldn't get Walter on the phone. Chad had said that I should ask him about the argument, and I meant to do just that. It was a Saturday, so I hiked to the soccer field, searching. I went up and down the fields, looking for Walter's usual team.

Eventually some of his friends called out to me. They had talked to Walter, but he had decided not to come, they said, casually juggling the ball between themselves. He hadn't told them why.

So I set myself for the long walk back. I cut through to the other side of the park, the rougher side where Walter had shown me the prostitutes and pointed out the transvestite.

The sight of Walter's motorcycle took me by surprise. It was parked just off the sidewalk, on the grass, and I remember thinking it strange to see a red Kawasaki, one just like Walter's, until I recognized his leather bag hanging from the back. Walter's back was to me, but I recognized the set of his stance, feet slightly apart, weight evenly distributed, shoulders square. He was talking to a woman in a white dress.

I couldn't hear what they were saying, but the woman threw her head back and laughed. There was something self-conscious in the gesture. I didn't have to move closer to know she was really a man, a man in a dress with fake blond hair and false eyelashes. It was clear, too, that they were flirting. Walter put a hand on her arm, inclined his head, moved closer to steal a kiss. I turned away, looking for a way to cross the street and duck into the woods without being seen.

Once out of sight behind some trees, I stopped. A couple walked past, holding hands, and I stared at them unblinking. I felt as if I were just waking up.

Gradually, though, things began to fall into place. The fact that Walter had friends I had never met. The way we'd both admired Chad in Rome. Walter had always been charming without being sexual, affectionate but from a distance, as if not wanting to get too close.

I crossed the park quickly and walked until I couldn't walk any farther. On a tiny street just behind the church of San Lorenzo, I passed a restaurant where they roasted chicken over open flames. The smell alone was enough to blot out the rest of the day, long enough for me to order some meat and zucchini, roasted asparagus, and small red potatoes. I sat at a small table, hunched over the food. I ate and ate and ate, my hands and lips greasy with animal fat. I washed it down with tap water and couldn't help but wish for wine.

I didn't need anymore to ask Walter what had happened on the ski trip, why he and Chad seemed to be at each other's throats.

※

It was raining the day it occurred to me that I might be pregnant. Counting back on my fingers, I realized I had lost my period somewhere between Jack's visit and my search for Walter at the soccer field. It had to be stress, I whispered to myself—not enough green vegetables and too little sleep. But I knew that wasn't true.

Chad and I had taken precautions, and I thought they had been good enough. But maybe our fingers had slipped, maybe we had touched something we shouldn't have, and then we touched each other. Or, perhaps, it had been more elemental than that. My body had wanted to be connected to his so fiercely that despite the barriers a child was conceived. My organs had leaned into his and coaxed out the impossible. Maybe it was a simple fact, that in the face of so much death my body was thirsting for life.

I watched the drops of rain gathering in heavy lines on the eaves until they fell, making perfect circles on the sidewalk below. The downpour silenced the city. Water backed up over the roads. A soaked pigeon walked across the cobblestones, pecking vainly in the cracks for grubs.

I breathed a cloud of fog onto the window, as if that would create a mist I could escape into, so I could become a fugitive, a thief. Then the clouds passed and the sky cleared, leaving the street shimmering in the light. I unbuttoned the top of my jeans and placed my hands over the pasta-rich roundness of my belly. I imagined it bigger and full of water and tissue and blood. I held the baby, there by the window, and watched the last raindrops fall.

✳

Several days later, I arrived at my studio to find my door open. I lingered in the doorway, afraid to see my property broken and scattered all over the floor. It didn't occur to me until I saw the expensive jacket over the back of the sofa that my prowler might be Walter.

"Shit," I said, when I realized what had happened. I dropped my backpack on the floor. "You scared me."

His white hand appeared first on the arm of the sofa, then his eyes, just over the edge. His hair stood straight up on end. He blinked once, twice, as if struggling to remember where exactly he was.

"I fell asleep," he muttered. "What time is it?"

"How did you get in?"

"You don't want to know." He sat up slowly.

I took a step or two closer to the sofa. "What are you doing here?"

"I pay for it. You'd think I could stop by once in a while."

His voice sounded dead and mean. A quick glance at my desk showed he hadn't moved anything, or if he had then he had put everything back with a meticulousness of which he didn't seem quite capable.

"What happened?" I asked.

"So we're still pretending we don't know?"

He stood up, his color patchy, as if parts of his face had lost their flow of blood and his lips were bruised, mashed into his face until the edges bled like lipstick into white skin. He hobbled over to the sink and bent over to one side, as if favoring one set of ribs.

"What are you talking about?" I asked.

Walter let the water run cold. His hand shook as he held the glass there, under the stream. "You know exactly what I'm talking about. The last time we saw each other. In the park?" He drank the entire glass of water and set about filling it again. "You were wearing a white sweater. You were kind of hard to miss."

I swallowed, filled with a sense of shame about the whole thing, even though I hadn't set about to spy on him. "I thought the same thing about your motorcycle."

Walter put the glass down and glanced across the room at the portraits. If I had known he was coming, I might have put them under blankets. We were past the point when I felt comfortable giving him a private viewing. His eyes narrowed, his neck craned, and he stared, as if trying to place where he'd seen them before. "So those are what you've been working so hard on?"

His voice was sarcastic, but I refused to take the bait. We had enough to argue about already. I thought about what I had seen, remembered how tall the prostitute had been. "Have you been to a doctor?"

Walter hobbled back over to the couch. "I just drank too much last night, that's all."

There was obviously more to his pain than a hangover, but it wasn't worth saying so. For all I knew, he had been through it before and had healed perfectly fine. "Let me at least make you some coffee," I said.

It took a few minutes for the water to boil. Walter stared wordlessly at the paintings until I put the cup down in front of him. He pointed to Saint Teresa, captured in her moment of doubt. "She looks a little bit like the way I feel."

"Walter . . ."

"I miss him," he said.

I didn't have to ask who he was talking about. "You told him, on your trip. Didn't you?"

Walter nodded. "I knew it wouldn't do any good." Then his mouth twisted in a grotesque shape and he folded his arms, unfolded them, ultimately leaving them helpless at his sides. He stared up at the ceiling with wet, shining eyes.

In that moment I knew for sure that Walter was in

love with Chad as surely and as passionately as I was. Maybe I could have comforted him by saying that nothing had changed, but it wouldn't have been the truth. Besides, the baby inside of me had stolen my last measure of sympathy. I needed every bit of energy for myself.

Sun streaming in through the frame of my window created a checkerboard pattern across the sofa. I followed the lines with my eyes, dividing the space into light and dark. Walter and I sat on a patch in between.

✳

Frank had always said that the pregnancy terrified my mother. She had had no husband, no prospects, no job. Still, perhaps there was something he'd missed, her private delight at what her body could achieve. That must have been some comfort to her.

Or maybe that thought had simply become a comfort to me. Each night I lay in the bath, my ears underwater, listening to the world as if through amniotic fluid. With closed eyes, I imagined spinal columns and embryos, cells dividing in a microscopic world. My daughter, before she had words, before she had lips, whispered to me. I heard her voice and knew she was a girl. To her, I was the sun, the moon, and the stars. My body made up her dark and formless world. I promised her safety, and in turn she vowed to give me unconditional love.

The guy behind the counter at the student dining hall handed Chad two sandwiches. We wound our way to the back, through brightly colored tables that had been arranged and rearranged by students. The only open table was a small sticky one in the very corner, butting up against the pinball machine where a kid who looked about twelve was pounding on the sides, trying to make it tilt.

"Sorry," Chad said.

"This is fine," I replied, as I squeezed in behind the table to sit on a narrow bench. "But we do need to talk."

It wasn't the time or the place to tell Chad about the baby, but it was becoming increasingly hard to get time with him. He blamed it on an upcoming set of exams, but that didn't fully explain it. He could've studied in the studio, where it was quiet, but instead he chose the library, or the living rooms of other friends who could help him with his work. Unlike me, they knew the answers to his questions.

"I have something important I need to tell you," I said.

Before I could continue, a woman had called his name. She made her way toward us, holding her sandwich over the crowd. She was wearing horn-rimmed glasses and a red wool cardigan embroidered down the front.

"Anika, this is Joanna."

We shook hands, smiling. She pushed her glasses back up on her nose. "Are you a friend of Chad's from home?"

"We met here," I said. "A couple of months ago."

"Your great misfortune," she said, laughing. She had just the barest hint of an accent, a slight roll to her r. Chad made a face. She returned it.

"How did the interview go?" she asked him.

"What interview?" I asked.

Chad looked at me briefly, then back at his sandwich. "Nothing, really."

"Nothing!" Anika laughed. "As if everyone else isn't ready to slit your throat. Chad is the only one of us who has a real live senator knocking on his door."

I should've known from the minute I saw her that she would be the bearer of bad tidings.

"It's not that big of a deal," he said. "I'd be a glorified messenger boy. And I probably won't get it anyway."

"We're all wondering how you got the interview in the first place."

He shrugged. "My father has raised money for the senator. And he mentioned that I'd be graduating, that's all."

I nodded, trying to swallow a bite of my sandwich. "And this is in D.C.?"

"Yes."

"When would you go?"

The sounds of the crowd in the bar swelled chaotically in the silence. Chad cleared his throat. "Four months. Give or take. Right after school gets out."

I could tell by the way he wouldn't meet my eyes that it hadn't occurred to him to ask me to come along.

A few days later, Chad, Walter, and I met at the *osteria* for the last time. Chad wanted notes that Walter had borrowed from him. Walter wanted dinner. They had both called to ask me to come. In the wake of Walter's admission, I had become their neutral ground.

The heat and noise and rush of smells that had once made the place seem friendly now made it claustrophobic and overwhelming. I should've been hungry, but the pungent smell of roasting meat and garlic made my stomach turn. I held on to my glass of mineral water as if it were a life preserver.

"Where are my notes?" Chad asked Walter before we even had a chance to order.

"Can't that wait?" Walter asked, with a hint of desperation.

"The test is tomorrow. I need to have them," Chad said.

I heard the unforgiving tone of his voice and saw the look on Walter's face, as if he had been slapped, and I knew there was no going back to the days when the three of us could sit at this table for hours. Chad would never be able to relax, Walter wouldn't be able to hide. Within five minutes, the two of them were yelling at each other. When Walter slammed the notebook on the table, Chad took it and left. I followed him out onto the sidewalk.

Chad shoved the notes in his backpack. "I don't believe how arrogant he is."

"Did you have to be so harsh?" I asked.

"Listen." He pulled out a wool scarf and wound it around his neck. "I know you're mad about the interview. I was going to tell you about it. It's just that I didn't have a chance. I swear."

"He was right. That you used him. You knew exactly how he felt about you and you went on that trip anyway. At least admit it."

"Maybe I did." Chad looked at me. "But what about you? How can you possibly judge me when you take so much of his money yourself?"

"I genuinely like Walter."

"You think I don't?" Chad shook his head. "And maybe I should be able to handle it better. But I'm doing the best I can." He took my hand, kissed me on the cheek. "I really do have to study. But we'll be able to sort it all out in a couple of days. After midterms. I promise."

I nodded, but I didn't believe him. After midterms there would be finals, and after finals he would be gone.

✳

When I went back inside, Walter had two shot glasses in front of him; one full, one empty. He filled mine with Scotch when I sat down.

"I understand the attraction," Walter said, "but you're being kind of stupid about the whole thing. Do you think you can trust him?"

It annoyed me that I had just gone outside to defend him and he didn't seem to feel any gratitude. "I'll stick to water, thanks," I said.

"Fine." Walter downed his drink and then held up mine in a mock toast. "To success in the art world."

The smell of it made my stomach turn over. "He didn't mean to hurt you."

"As if you give a shit," he said.

When I walked out, Walter didn't catch up with me until I was already at the bus stop. I imagined he stayed long enough to down another shot of whiskey, to drop some money on the table, to exit casually as if nothing in the world were wrong.

"Let me give you a ride home," he said.

Not only was it too cold to be on the back of a motor-cycle, he could barely stand up. "Are you kidding?"

"Okay. I'm sorry for what I said. I'm an asshole."

"Maybe you just shouldn't be around him for a while."

Walter leaned forward, so close that I could smell the garlic on his breath. He lowered his voice to an almost whisper, caught my wrist in his left hand. "You still think this is just about him."

"What else?"

"What else." He squeezed my wrist until it just began to hurt, then he dropped it abruptly, as if the skin had grown hot. "Maybe it's about being normal. Maybe about having friends who know what you are, and who aren't ashamed of it."

"I'm not ashamed of you."

"Is that why you ran away? It looked like ashamed to me." Walter stepped back and didn't let me answer. "Do you want to know how many girls he's slept with since the beginning of the school year?"

"Shut up."

"Fine." Walter half-turned, as if he were about to walk off. "Fuck you. You know? Really. I would've loved you more than he ever did."

Walter looked as if he might grab me again, this time by the throat. I saw it in his eyes, the potential for violence, the fact that he could not control what came into his head or out of his mouth. Fear welled up inside me, a flash of adrenaline that told me in no uncertain terms to get away.

My bus pulled up and I bolted up the stairs onto it. The only other passenger stared at me, stared out the window at Walter.

"Joanna!" I heard him wail as the door was closing, suddenly accommodating, suddenly drunkenly sweet. I realized I was breathing heavily, and I knew that I might not sleep that night, that I might not sleep again, ever. Walter slapped the window with an open hand.

The bus began to move. I watched as he took a step alongside it, then two, then three, leaping to make sure I knew he was there, to make sure I was witness to this manic dance. When the bus picked up speed, Walter did the same, pumped his arms until he was sprinting. I looked away and am not sure how long he kept it up before he had to peel off, left there in the road, drunk and doubled-up and panting.

*

Chad came to my studio to explain about the job interview, and we ended up making love. Walter found us there, together. He didn't knock the way he should have, but just opened the door, arms full of flowers, as if we were still in the days when he came and went as he pleased.

I wrapped the sheet around me. Chad stood up from the couch, bare-chested, wearing sweatpants. I saw it in Walter's eyes, the hurt when confronted with proof that there was no room for him anymore.

I couldn't move nearly fast enough to prevent the fight. Walter charged at Chad, head down and arms out. He knocked Chad back, over the box that served as a coffee table, which collapsed under Chad's weight, sending papers and books flying. Walter fell on top of Chad, trying to pin him down.

Chad rolled over before Walter could establish a good hold. Chad stood up, took a step away, but Walter scrambled to get at his legs. Chad grabbed Walter's hair and he brought his knee up to meet Walter's face. The bones came together with a sickening crunch. Blood splattered across the floor. Chad lifted Walter's head up to hit him again, and that's when I began to scream, a high-pitched voice I didn't recognize as my own.

When I grabbed Chad's arm, he let go, pushing Walter away from him. Walter must have picked up a pair of needle-nosed pliers because I heard Chad swear as I held him, and then I heard the awful fiber tear of thick canvas as Walter attacked the painting of Saint Teresa.

This isn't the worst thing that could happen, I remember thinking. Awful things happen all the time. This isn't that bad.

But when I turned I saw my mother's face after the car accident, after they had pulled her out of the wreckage by the side of the river. Her desperation slammed into me, the crush of steel against her rib cage. I sat down—I had no choice. My knees buckled under me and I couldn't shake the feeling that I was in two places at once, both with Walter and in a place I had never been, seeing something I had never seen, had never imagined, had never wanted to see. The face in the painting, the face of my mother, had gone through the windshield and broken wide open, her bones and her soul bathed in blood.

I don't remember closing my eyes, but by the time I opened them a few seconds later Walter had already reached the door, one hand holding his nose. Great gobs of magenta fell onto the floor, marking his way.

Chad knelt down and put a warm hand on my back. He kissed me on the cheek, on the top of my head, and I could feel the plump, blood-rich wall of my uterus begin to separate, the placenta breaking down.

"Are you all right?" he asked.

"I need to go home," I said. "Can you help me get home?"

"Of course," Chad answered and held my hand, put his arm protectively around me on the bus, unaware that I was losing what would have been our child.

✳

I spent that evening curled up in the bottom of the shower. The water came down in a scalding cascade, but I couldn't stay warm. I tried in vain to gather the clots together, to hold them with wrinkled fingers so they wouldn't slip down the drain.

Naked and on my knees, my forehead up against the edge of the porcelain tub, I begged for the bleeding to stop. I begged for someone to help me, for my mother, for God, for Jack.

The miscarriage hurt, physically, as if someone were wringing my uterus in two tightly clenched fists. And I was terrified, the way I was stepping into a confessional for the first time, to close the door behind me and face the evidence of my own faults. I had brought it on myself, the miscarriage, because I had taken advantage of Walter, and because I had slept with Chad.

I had given up Jack, when I should have held on.

Calmly and quietly, Chad and I broke off our relationship. We met on the steps of Piazzale Michelangelo one blustery day, when our words were buffeted by wind. We stared at the city rather than at each other, at the buildings that hadn't changed over hundreds and hundreds of years.

We talked about many things that day, but I didn't mention the miscarriage. Chad, in turn, did not mention love.

TWELVE

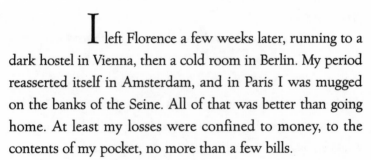

I left Florence a few weeks later, running to a dark hostel in Vienna, then a cold room in Berlin. My period reasserted itself in Amsterdam, and in Paris I was mugged on the banks of the Seine. All of that was better than going home. At least my losses were confined to money, to the contents of my pocket, no more than a few bills.

My wandering lasted six months. Eventually, I ended up on the Lower East Side of New York City, in a building owned by Lena's godson. I lived in a basement apartment. Despite the fact that it got no daylight and my bathroom had no door, the super kept the front-door locks working and garbage out of the hall. I wouldn't say I was happy, but at least I had found a place where I could begin to get by. It made me feel better to put up a bookshelf, and I kept Lena's book on the lives of the saints next to my bed.

In October I sat with my neighbors on our stoop, watching city volunteers plant trees. When I had moved in, there was nothing on the street but cement and wrought-iron banisters, abandoned cars and graffiti on trash cans. It was as if the neighborhood reflected the bleakness in my heart. The only bit of green was crabgrass growing in the cracks of the sidewalks, a scrawny dandelion breaking through a chink in the stoop.

I held Nia, the four-year-old who lived on the first floor. Her mother Janele stood two steps above. Nia had her brown arms over my knees, her small body pressed tightly up against mine.

Next door, Eddie and Estelle had their window open, resting their elbows on the sill. Eddie never tired of telling us they'd been in the neighborhood since Eisenhower. Estelle was forever leaving things by my basement window that she thought I might want—a dying philodendron in a wicker basket, a bottle of cheap champagne her kids left after New Year's Eve.

Eddie predicted the maple trees wouldn't survive. They did look fragile, leafless and vulnerable on this hard street. He listed a number of beautification projects that had come and gone, murals on the corner, a community garden on the vacant lot. "Someone comes and screws it up," he said. "Or they leave it half-finished in the first place."

"At least they're trying," I said.

Eddie chewed on his cigar as if it were a wad of gum. "Their kind of trying doesn't get you anywhere."

Janele held out a hand to her daughter. "C'mon girl," she said. "We have to do something about that head of yours." Nia's black hair had been straightened for a birthday party, but her tiny fingers had worked it free from its bow.

When the truck drove off, Eddie and Estelle closed their window. And I stayed sitting out on the stoop, staring at the trees that had no leaves, watching them as it grew dark.

*

Eight months after I left Florence, I got a job working in a kitchen. We catered fancy parties uptown, served cocktails and hors d'oeuvres on silver trays. I washed lettuce. I polished silver. I carved roses out of radishes. If I'd been my grandfather, after twelve hours of such work I would've walked the twenty blocks across town to save the subway fare. I wasn't quite that self-sacrificing. When I ran out of money, I used my credit card.

I blamed Walter and Chad in equal measure for the position in which I found myself. New York was a good place to do that, because it was as far away from God and a natural world as I could get. I did not have to be particularly honest, not with their memories, not with myself.

At work I took up with a chef named Aaron who thought he was David Bowie. And he might have been if Bowie had come from New Jersey, if he were Jewish, if he'd had black hair. Those were the only differences between them, Aaron told me, but I disagreed. I had actually heard Aaron sing.

The two of us took breaks together and stood out on the sidewalk through the frigid winter. He smoked; I drank black coffee. We both chewed peppermint gum on the way back in, trying to get rid of the bitterness on our tongues.

Aaron was a painter who specialized in emaciated men with weird skin tones. He had a back bedroom full of canvases that were tall and narrow, shaped like Gothic windows. And in each frame a man was trapped against a white background, his face filled with apprehension. Aaron depicted their bodies in loving detail, wasted as they were by various stages of AIDS.

We both agreed that neither one of us stood a commercial chance. The hot property that year was a man named Little Bear, a Crow from Montana. The first time I read anything about him was in *The New Yorker*. He played drums in the morning in Central Park—that's what the article was about, not his visuals or the content of his work, but that this man gathered white people around him in a circle. The *New York Times Magazine* included him in a photo shoot chronicling America's most creative minds under thirty. He wore black, the way they all did in the picture, but Little Bear was the only one with braids.

＊

Coming home from the kitchen one night, I pushed open the door of my apartment to find a letter from Jack on the floor. It arrived inside a letter from Lena, who had written a note in her clear hand, beautiful Italian on a cream-colored card. The reason she was writing, she said, was because she'd received some mail after I'd left. She hoped I was well.

Jack didn't put his return address on the outside of the envelope, so certain he was that the letter would not need to be returned. I recognized his handwriting, the haphazard way he printed my name.

I placed the envelope on my table, a heavy piece of furniture that would've fit eight, had I owned that many chairs, had I known that many people. It marked my one real accomplishment since arriving in the city, a daring rescue from an alley, followed by a three-day repair on the legs. The table held Jack's letter so that I didn't have to—I could circle around it, hands free, chewing on a piece of ice.

I opened it eventually, slitting through the top of the envelope with a butter knife, to find that Jack was dating a woman named Kayla. He mentioned that in the first paragraph, as if there were nothing between the two of us that might make him hesitate to admit it to me. He sent pictures of the two of them on their vacation, as if I were his sister, his cousin, his friend.

I stared at them, finding it hard to recognize Jack or his expression, a dumb smile that had nothing to do with me. His hair had grown longer, his Eddie Bauer flannel shirts a cut above his usual Salvation Army. His boots looked expensive. They were heavy-soled, with red laces.

I thought a lot about that news, carried the letter with me on my way to work, home from the library where I checked out books on Lenore Tawney and Camille Claudel. I tried to see only him in those photographs, to imagine myself there, on the snow-covered slopes of Mt. Rainier. As hard as I tried to ignore her, that girl crept in, tucked underneath his arm, her face shining, her hair beautifully combed, her small hands firmly clasped around his waist.

Mercifully, the letter fell out of the back of my sketchbook one afternoon, part of an accident involving two plates, a glass of water, and a piece of pie that made the Polish waitress laugh until she cried. The ink inside the letter bled right off the paper, a blue wash diffusing the details of Jack's life through the ice water, across the table, and into the whipped cream on the pie.

In May, the *Times* ran a story about a priest who performed miracles. There was a picture of him, a small man from El Salvador. In the photograph he stood with both hands on the head of a little girl. From the amount of white lace on her dress, it had to have been the occasion of her first communion.

"Janele," I called out. I was sitting with her and Aaron on the stoop, the newspaper divided between the three of us. Janele had a pen in her hand, tackling the crossword. Down on the sidewalk, Nia was drawing with colored chalk directly onto the cement.

"Your priest is in the paper," I said.

She didn't go to church every Sunday. There were too many late Saturday nights for that, too many shifts during the week when she couldn't see Nia. But she brought me specially prepared dishes to commemorate Holy Week and kept palms behind the crucifix on her kitchen wall.

"Padre Sandoval?" She took the section of the paper and scanned it. "Oh." She handed it back to me, as if I had disappointed her. "The miracles."

Nia drew green lines that curved from the bottom of our stairs out to the base of the trees that had sprouted tender young leaves. In the soft light of morning, she moved in and out of shadow, adding perfectly round blossoms, globes of white and blue.

"They say he heals people."

"They've been saying that for years. There are people around the church all the time, asking for favors. I know someone once who asked him to cure her arthritis. He told her to say a Hail Mary and then sent her home. Eighty-seven years old and she can still wash her kitchen floor on her hands and knees."

"Big miracle," Aaron laughed, but Janele shook her head at him.

"It's true. She doesn't have pain. She lives in her own house. She can do something she couldn't do ten years ago. It gives her pride to take care of herself. And that's something."

We drifted back into the paper. I read the story about the priest, Aaron looking over my shoulder. Two people were featured: a woman who'd had late-stage breast cancer that went into spontaneous remission, and a man who swore that he could walk after a mountain-biking accident had left him paralyzed from the chest down. Both of those people attributed their cure to Padre Sandoval. So did their doctors. And the reporter stressed Father Sandoval's giving nature, the way he responded to children at the Catholic school, the habit he had of literally taking off his clothing to give it to men on the street.

The comments of other priests in the diocese gave the impression that it was difficult to be in the presence of Father Sandoval, that his sanctity could go a bit too far. It could be embarrassing, one admitted, to walk down the street with a cheerful half-naked man.

As for the fuss over the miracles, the healer himself dismissed it. "I pray for the intercession of our Blessed Mother," he said. "And that is all I do."

*

In the middle of summer, Aaron walked into the kitchen. He wore black leather and had an earring in one nostril. He was trying to look tough, but he was too thin for that. I was standing over a bucket of peeled potatoes, carving them into a hundred tiny angels. He paused at my hip, shaking his head. I looked down at my T-shirt, splattered with backwash water, a stained apron tied around my waist.

"What?"

"You got better clothes than that?"

"Better clothes for what?"

He threw his jacket over a chair and started to wash his hands. Unlike most of the chefs, Aaron scrubbed with the precision of a surgeon, each finger, the back of the hands, up over the wrists.

"To go talk to Paula."

"And she is?"

"The curator for the show I'm in."

Aaron had already told me about it—five artists in a vacant storefront before it was converted into a restaurant.

"Hector, who seems to paint nothing but reproductions of *People* magazine covers, has decided our venture is beneath him." Aaron wiped his hands on a paper towel. "Or more to the point, Paula decided he is beneath us."

"So she's looking for someone?"

I had been experimenting with wooden coffee stirrers, filched by the boxful from the stock room. Using wood glue as mortar, I had built a scale replica of Brunelleschi's dome. It sat in the corner of my apartment collecting dust.

"I told her you would bring your portfolio by this afternoon."

I looked down at the bucket at my feet. Sixty-two angels by last count. We needed one hundred. "I don't see how I can."

"Aren't you feeling sick? I'm pretty sure I saw you throw up. It wouldn't be advisable for you to be around food."

I put down my knife, began to undo my apron. "You are a piece of work, Aaron."

"You got that right."

✳

The second letter from Jack arrived on the same day as my quarterly report from the rental agency handling the farm in Bright River. It was a coincidence, getting the two envelopes the same day, because both of them dealt with the same subject.

"Stopped by the place to look around," Jack wrote.

"Still seems to be in pretty good shape. Living room and bedrooms look fine. The barn might be leaking in the back."

That was a set of images I couldn't easily dismiss. Jack stepping out of his truck to open the front gate. Jack heading up the stairs to the front porch. Jack with his hands around his eyes, trying to cut out any reflection from the window. I wondered whether he took the trail up to the reservoir or drove his car out to the river.

He didn't mention his girlfriend at all, just the trip to Bright River and some details about his job. Balancing my checkbook that night, I wove an elaborate fantasy around the idea of a trip to Seattle, where Jack and I would walk through the campus of the university under the canopy of cedar trees. I wanted to see mountains, I wanted to be with him, in the car, in the grocery store, wherever he was. I wanted things to be back to normal, the way they had always been.

✳

Around Christmas, I was in a second show. That one featured two paintings and a freestanding sculpture, a scale model replica of Frank's barn out of coffee stirrers aged in tea and salt water. The barn led to the paragraph in the *New York Times* that described it as an "artistic harkening back to good old days, simple country realism after the glitz of the eighties." When people passed it, they mur-

mured that they'd never seen anything like it. I felt like asking them where the hell they'd lived.

The review led to a few phone calls right afterward, phone calls that got my hopes up but put no money in my pocket. Well-dressed men and women paraded through my dark apartment—one couple even took me out for coffee. They poked and prodded, then left me at the table wearing clothes that were too formal for the rest of my life.

✳

Eddie would've been the first one to admit he was wrong about the trees. Nia learned to mark the seasons by them, yellow and red leaves in the fall, green seed spinners strewn across the sidewalk in the spring. She planted the seeds in milk cartons and they grew too.

Nia finished first grade, then second. I celebrated my twenty-fifth birthday with margaritas on the Staten Island Ferry. Around that time, Little Bear's career fell apart when he made an ill-thought-out reference to his Indian heritage. "Nothing," he was quoted as saying, "ever came off that reservation except for dirt." Aaron and I smirked when we found out his real name was Norman and he wasn't Indian at all.

M y first meeting with Graham Easton, the gallery owner, took place in a restaurant on the Upper West Side, a few blocks from Lincoln Center. I brought my portfolio, but Mr. Easton didn't bother to look at it. "We've already been watching you for some time," he said with a wave of his hand. "This is more of a chance for you to get to know me, to get to know us."

He was a heavyset man, well-dressed and capable of handling more than one task at a time. Even as we chatted, he casually canvassed the room to see who else was there.

"What are you working on now?" he asked eventually.

"Portraits of children," I said, because I had been drawing Nia as often as I could.

He nodded. "Interesting. We would definitely want to consider those. If we sign you."

I stared at the orange on the side of his plate. It had been carved by hand and delicately placed in counterpoint to the salmon fettuccine, the greens. He was discussing my future as an artist, but I couldn't get past that orange, the curve of it, the flecks of white on the skin. It was beautiful, that piece of fruit, a work of art, a labor of love.

At the end of the meal, Graham Easton bit into it. An obscene squirt of juice ran down his chin.

In Central Park, I watched the way the children played together and alone, the girls who stuck to the swings and the slides, the boys who crawled into the bushes. A brown-haired girl ate popcorn with the delicacy of a bird. A boy yelled at the top of his lungs to a playmate who was standing right next to him. In the middle of a light rain, a toddler collapsed into tears. He lay screaming under the edge of the slide while his teenage baby-sitter pleaded with him to come out.

Aaron had lent me a camera with a couple of lenses. I learned to fade into the background, turning at the last moment as if I intended to take the photograph of someone else. That way, I caught the children without smiles. Some of them looked so young, and as Aaron developed the photographs it seemed to me that they would stay that way, bright-eyed and smooth-skinned—the teenagers who everyone trusts, the elderly who don't seem to get wrinkles. Others seemed preternaturally old. It was in their eyes, the worried way they concentrated on play, on rocks, on the sandwiches they'd been given. Some, with wild hair and rips in their collars, were impossible to place either way.

I tacked the pictures of the children up on the walls of my apartment. The first time Nia saw them she tried to peel them off the plaster. It was as if she'd been an only child and was being confronted with the presence of siblings she'd never know existed. She ripped one into tiny pieces and was sent by Janele back upstairs to their apartment, where she stomped around so vehemently that we could not hold a conversation. Janele smiled grimly.

"Strong-willed child," she said.

* * *

The third letter from Jack said he had asked Kayla to marry him. I threw it out almost immediately, dropped it in the can on Eddie's stoop as I ran to the subway. I was late for a meeting with Graham, where we were supposed to hammer out the terms and conditions for my first solo show. Once underground, I sat on the train, staring at my own reflection in the black window. I pretended not to feel much at all.

* * *

The children wanted to be smaller than the saints, paler in color and yet more intense. I cut the field of vision—no shoulders, no ears, no tops of heads, until all that was left were the eyes and bits of noses, glimpses of cheeks and chins. I sanded ten boards the size of paperback books into smooth rectangles. They were surprisingly weighty to the touch.

I felt faint echoes of the passion I had experienced in Florence. Having been in love with a series once, the second time I was more tentative, a reluctant surrender rather than a wholehearted plunge into the kind of madness I'd experienced before. I managed the children in three-hour spurts, binges interrupted by shifts in the kitchen, or meals with Janele.

The process seemed manageable, logical even, until I got to the last one, the final child, a girl of about eight years old, with matted hair. I couldn't remember taking her photograph or seeing her mother and yet she was there, on my table, with thin pinched lips, white Irish skin, and jet black eyebrows. I began her portrait on a Friday afternoon. That night I couldn't sleep, staring at the Dickensian expression in her eyes, the hint of despair as if she were all on her own on a freezing street corner, forced to beg.

The more I looked at her, the more I felt drawn in, until the other children paled in comparison, even Nia, which didn't make any sense, because Nia was the one child I actually knew. But there was something else in the eyes of the strange girl, a quality that transcended physical knowing.

On Saturday I cut new boards; on Sunday I painted. On Monday and Tuesday I took vacation time that I'd intended to use on Martha's Vineyard. I stacked the portraits of the other children and placed them in a box under the table, experimented with names for the girl as I changed the angle of her face, the nature of her expression. I worked better and steadier in that four days than I had in years.

It took Aaron to see what I could not. He came over one night, and while we were drinking he peered at the girl in her many incarnations. The air still smelled vaguely of turpentine, and blue paint residue lingered under the corners of my nails.

"You never told me you had a daughter," he said.

"I don't."

"Well, who's that then?"

I coughed inadvertently, then it became terribly important to draw him out of the room, to stop him from looking at her. I shrugged on my jacket and I picked up my house keys. I started talking about something completely unrelated to the subject of children and I rattled on, using short words, quick words, any words that were not about the girl I had painted. It wasn't until I couldn't find my left shoe, until I was down on my hands and knees, searching for it under my bed, that I started to cry.

Aaron pulled me up from the floor and my hands were dirty, smeared with dust from under the bed. I inadvertently rubbed them across my face, trying to wipe away tears as even more came, enough to soak Aaron's shirt where he held me.

I should not have wanted the baby, but I had. I had wanted to wrap her in blankets and keep her warm, to feed her the milk from my breast the way I wanted to be fed by my mother.

Aaron wrapped a sweater around me and led me to the edge of my bed. I had no couch, so we sat on flannel sheets and twisted blankets. We didn't go out that night, or the next. Aaron made me coffee laced with brandy that he borrowed from Janele.

A₅ the date for the show neared, I developed an ache in my left shoulder. The strain of the past few months condensed into a hard knot that hid up under the shoulder blade. Pain began to wear on me until all I could think about was getting rid of it. I bought ibuprofen in bulk, and drank bourbon over ice, just enough to dull the anxiety.

I didn't answer my phone while I was working. I turned the ringer off and let the machine swallow Graham's words. "You need a cellular phone," he said more than once. "I can't get hold of you when I need to."

I chewed pills throughout the day and took more at night when I listened to his messages. I waited until I was sure he had left the gallery, then picked up the phone to talk to his machine. I told him my shoulder hurt. The next call, he offered me the number of an orthopedist I couldn't afford.

✳

Rain turned the city gray, washed the streets a dark and somber color. But everything in the gallery was white, bright white, dry white, as if weather didn't have the slightest bearing on its important business.

When I arrived, dressed in my fisherman's sweater and soft pants, I dripped all over the wood floor. The reception-ist offered to take my jacket and carried it away at arm's length from her silk skirt.

Peter, the man heading up the crew who would hang the paintings, met me with a crowbar in his hand. He'd been the one to call me when the crate arrived from Florence, but he had no way of knowing what he was asking me to do—to look at work that had long since been buried.

It worried me that the paintings might not be as powerful as I remembered. Without the contents of the crate, I still had the children I'd painted, the architectural models, a few other experiments here and there. But Graham had made it clear that the financial center of the show would be the saints. They were large, eye-catching, unique. I wished I had his confidence in them.

Peter offered me the crowbar, but I didn't trust myself to take it. After he had pried the top off, he handed me a letter that sat on top of the paintings, a card addressed in Tomas's spidery handwriting. I took off my clogs and put the letter inside them. I wanted to be able to feel the floor with my toes.

Tomas had marked each painting with masking tape and a permanent marker. First I pulled out Rose of Lima, lime-scarred and carrying the weight of hell in her eyes. I took the fabric from around her and laid her up against the wall. She alone had enough power to change the neutral tone in the room, the untouched feeling of white walls. She seemed to suck in the light around her, to turn it into even brighter color for herself.

I saw the shake of Peter's head, not too far from vanity to smile a little, to imagine the shake of a hundred heads at the opening, the surprise of each elegant adult calmly eating hors d'oeuvres only to round a partition to come face-to-face with her. Rose would make them choke on their shrimp, spit back up into their cocktail napkins.

Peter unwrapped one, then another, then a third, and propped them up against the wall. Catherine and Margaret and Bernadette made me stand up straight. They had a delicacy that I had never seen, a gold-leaf pattern setting off the expressions in their eyes. I didn't know what Peter saw, how anyone else would interpret them, but what I saw was my younger self, as clearly as if I had been looking at a photograph.

It was hard to believe that I had ever been so happy, had ever been so excited as to be able to create those faces. I felt affection for the woman who I once was, the woman who fell in love with Chad and Walter. With that affection came sorrow over what I had lost. I knew there would be more opportunities to sit and drink wine, long hours and days to be in love. Still, I felt like crying over the mistakes I had made in Italy.

"There's one more," Peter said, pulling a wrapped canvas from the box. His voice shook me out of myself.

"No. That's it."

He read the masking-tape label. "Teresa of Avila."

"She can't be shown," I said automatically. "She was ruined." I had forgotten a lot of things about those paintings, but not the jagged rip in her face.

"Shouldn't we at least look? Maybe we can fix it."

I shook my head. I had just seen a glimpse of my younger self. I didn't want to lose her all over again.

*

I'm not quite sure what brought me back to the gallery a few days before the show. Graham didn't want me there, he had made it clear. He had collected the merchandise from me and wanted none of my opinions about its presentation or marketing. The major decisions had long been taken out of my hands.

I walked through the glass gallery doors to find Graham talking with a woman. She had perfect posture, was in her early fifties, and was wearing a full-length mink coat. At the sound of footsteps, she turned, but only halfway, as if few people were important enough to command her full attention. Graham stood with her over one of my paintings, laid flat on the floor in front of a blank space on the wall, an area highlighted by a special floodlight. Graham ducked his head, deferring to her.

I could see it in his eyes when I approached—fear splashed with annoyance, as if he were a parent and I were a child and I had caught him in a lie. He cut the distance between me and the woman, me and the painting, catching me halfway.

"Joanna."

"Graham."

"I thought we'd see you day after tomorrow."

"I thought I'd see how it was coming."

The woman turned to say something. That's when I realized they were looking at Saint Teresa.

"No," I said immediately. "No."

"We want her, Jo," Graham said. "The only question is where."

"She's not part of the contract." I wondered how they found her, how they knew she existed at all. I doubted Peter would've said anything. There wouldn't have been reason for him to tell.

"Actually," the woman walked over. "She is. We stipulated very clearly—the entire series from Florence. And she's one of that series."

"She's damaged."

"It adds something. It looks deliberate."

"It *was* deliberate."

"On the part of the artist, I mean." The woman tilted her head, slipping a slim box of Dunhill cigarettes out of her coat pocket. "It's an anticlerical statement. Or artistic frustration. Or madness—an attempt to destroy something so beautiful. It's controversy." She opened the box, placed a cigarette in her mouth.

"You can't."

"Artists usually fight to have their pieces in, not taken out."

Graham pulled a lighter out of his pocket and held his hand steady for her to touch the flame. When she inhaled, her cheeks became even higher, thinner, revealing the bone structure of a racehorse, or a champion greyhound.

"Who are you?" I asked.

She looked at Graham. He put the lighter away. "She owns the gallery, Joanna."

"I thought *you* owned the gallery," I said.

"My name is on it. She's the one who owns it."

The woman took a deep drag, blew the smoke up and out in a gesture that seemed oddly familiar. "Marguerite Haffner," she said, holding out a hand. "I believe you know my son Walter."

*

In the movies, Jack's news would have come to me in a telegram. Clark Gable would have sent one to Claudette Colbert and Zanuck would have held the shot long enough for the audience to read the message. WEDDING OFF STOP CAN'T LIVE WITHOUT YOU STOP MARRY ME STOP. There would've been a close-up on the heroine as grateful tears filled her eyes, as she brought a knuckle up to her mouth to bite it.

I didn't bite my knuckle. I didn't even cry. And the telegram was, in reality, a two-day delivery from Federal

Express. "I've left Kayla," was what Jack actually wrote. "It's a long story, but here's my new address." I read down to the end of the letter, which he closed with "I miss you."

He underlined those three words for emphasis. Stop.

✳

The miracle worker stood in the entryway of the church, near the font of holy water, where daylight began to give way to the darkness of the sanctuary. He was dressed for mass already, even though I arrived more than an hour early, the better to have silence and to pray. Father Sandoval was listening to a parishioner, an elderly man stooped over with scoliosis. The old man had the translucent skin of the elderly. In contrast, the priest's face seemed ageless, brown and unlined. He held one of the man's hands in two of his own. I imagined a confession, some serious words about repentance. What I heard, instead, as I walked by, was the elderly man saying, "So Saint Peter turns to God and . . ." The laughter of the priest echoed down the aisle.

I knelt in a pew a few rows back from the altar. The church has marble statues mounted in side grottoes, a benevolent Christ on one side, a gentle Madonna on the other. I closed my eyes to both of them. I didn't pray. I couldn't. The only thing that came to mind, the only prayer that came to my lips, was a plea for relief. I was afraid to open my eyes, afraid to let in the light and the beauty of the marble, because I knew it was meant for others—the elderly man who had made the priest laugh, the woman who was on the altar making preparations for the service. They were holy, I was not. My lost baby was proof enough of that.

The organist began to play as parishioners dribbled in, a few at first, then more as the hour drew near. By the time mass started, the church was full. The woman next to me clutched a rosary, whispered the prayers to Mary under her breath. There was so little space between us that I could see crumbs on her skirt. The temperature rose appreciably, and I understood why many of the men wore short-sleeved shirts. They knew Father Sandoval and the crowds at his masses. They brought their babies for him to bless, had petitions written on pieces of paper to place in the collection plate along with their donations.

The choir director raised her hands and the organist began to play at full volume. The congregation stood. A dark-haired boy of about twelve came down the center aisle, carrying a cross cast from bronze. A half step behind were another boy and a girl carrying white candles in bronze holders that matched the crucifix. All three wore sneakers under their robes, thick-soled tennis shoes with stripes on the side. After the children came the adults carrying the Bible.

At the end came Father Sandoval, eyes straight ahead, lips moving. On his face was an expression of absolute calm, as if whatever frightened other people did not frighten him. Women crossed themselves as he passed. A murmur rose from no specific direction, as if the walls had started to speak. The sound surrounded him like wind, and I felt myself, felt the building itself, lean in, just to be closer to where he walked.

The story of the woman with the hemorrhage came back to me as I stood there. That woman had heard Jesus was a healer, and she reached out to touch the hem of his garment. With that briefest of contact, the flow of blood stopped. Her faith, Christ declared, had made her whole.

Father Sandoval had not yet passed me, and all of a sudden I felt as if I had been asleep all that time and only just woken up. I held out my hand. It was the reach of a lover who realizes that all has been lost, the reach of a child who knows the parent will never return. I stretched out my hand across the emptiness of the aisle and brushed the material of his sleeve.

I don't know what the woman with the hemorrhage felt—a bolt of lightning, a surge of electricity, the opening of the heavens and the descent of a dove perhaps. What I did get was a dirty look from the woman in the pew in front of me. No one was supposed to step out of the confines of the pew, certainly not out into the empty space of the aisle.

Father Sandoval stopped. His retinue continued singing with everyone else and walked on toward the altar. There was no need for the priest to look around, to wonder who was touching him. He met my eyes directly, with no criticism or sense of hurry. It was as if the ceremony could go on around us, but we were protected in a sacred place.

"Go home," he said, then smiled so gently that it dried up the tears running down my cheeks.

And so I went. Walked out of the church, got into a cab, packed up the few things I wanted, gave the rest to Janele, except for my table, which Aaron had always coveted. I didn't realize until the next morning, as I handed the flight attendant my ticket and got ready to board the plane, that the pain in my shoulder had disappeared.

THIRTEEN

✳

✳

✳

✳

At Rene's, I unload a plastic tarp, four gallons of paint, rollers, and masking tape from the back of my truck onto the sidewalk. It hasn't snowed for a few days and the whole walk has long since been shoveled clean. Rene comes to the front door in shirtsleeves, her breath white in the December air. She puts her hand on one hip and asks me what the hell I am doing. Sometimes she plays at being the tough rancher's daughter. Sometimes I play back.

"What the hell does it look like I'm doing?" I shove past her, a gallon of paint in one hand, the tarp draped over the other.

"Being a smart-ass?" she answers as she walks behind the counter. I put the paint in the storage room, stacking everything over the tortilla chips and cans of beans.

"I thought your look could use an upgrade."

Rene stares at me as if she does not know who I am. It occurs to me that it is because for the first time in a long time I am not struggling. I wonder whether it shows in my face. I travel back to my conversation with Lena, the one in her kitchen over biscotti and sweet wine. I can see a stretch of highway running along the river. I have had loneliness. I am only just now beginning to see the possibilities.

"Joanna." There is warning in Rene's voice. She wants an explanation.

"Merry Christmas," I say, throwing color strips on her counter. "I'm thinking about basic cream with a periwinkle trim. That'll be neutral enough to show off the fresco on the back wall."

"Fresco?"

I take one of the photographs down from the wall. The frame is filthy, the surface of the glass covered with dust. It leaves a square where the paint is true yellow, in contrast to the faded corn color everywhere else.

"I'm going to take these," I say, brushing away the cobweb. "Do you have a box I can put them in?"

"Listen, Jo, I appreciate your wanting to do something, but . . ."

I walk back to the storeroom and grab an empty box myself. I stare at Rene for a minute, and she backs down. I know what she is about to say, that she's not sure my work is right for her place, that it's all well and good for New York and all, but her diners don't want to eat their steaks staring at bleached animal bones.

"Give me some credit."

She bites the side of a fingernail. "Is it going to be big?"

"Yes."

"Is it going to take long?"

"Decades." I pull off one picture, then another. "You will not get rid of me until the day I die." She smiles at that. "Seriously, let me do this for you."

Words do not come easily to me, and Rene knows it. It is almost impossible for me to talk about love, but I can easily finish a room. I am awkward with hugs, but I can do this one thing.

And Rene realizes it. She cocks her head, staring at me for a good long time. Suddenly, as if everything is settled, she moves behind the counter. "Do you want some breakfast?"

"I already ate," I say regretfully.

"The macaroni and cheese should come out of the oven soon. Maybe lunch?"

"That would be great."

Rene turns from me to begin loading dishes into the sink, but I know it is a cover so I can't see her smile. She doesn't want to scare me off, to send me back into my hermit house at the edge of the woods. But even though she tries to hide it, I know by the set of her shoulders that I have made her happy. In a few minutes she'll dial Chuck's number at the station and whisper to him all about it. Then I'll have the two of them inordinately pleased because I have chosen to do one small favor. As I work over the next few weeks, I will have to put up with sidelong smiling glances and plates of lasagna with green salad on the side. And that will be all right with me.

※

It is not late at night, but it gets so dark so early this time of year that it feels like midnight. I am sitting on the floor in the living room, the framed pictures from Rene's scattered across the floor. To begin working, I need to pull them from behind the glass so I can see the detail on the faces. In part, I just want to be closer to all of them, from the men who started the first general store to the Indians encased in Western dress, lined up in distressing rows in the missionary school at Fort Spokane.

I am staring at those pictures when the phone rings. The sound startles me, and when I move a piece of glass pops out of a frame, breaking into pieces. One slices across the fleshy pad of my left thumb. It starts bleeding immediately, even before it begins to hurt. Without thinking, I shake the thumb up and down, as if I had smashed it—sending an accidental spray of red droplets up over my head and onto the wall, across the carpet.

The phone keeps ringing, and in my shock over what has just happened I answer it.

"Joanna."

"Hmm," I say, wrapping the edge of my T-shirt around my thumb. I realize as I cover it that the cut winds from the top to the bottom and halfway around. If I look I might see down to the bone.

"This is Walter."

The truth of that statement, which should shock me at least a little after all this time, is nothing compared to the pain I am beginning to feel in my hand.

"I really cut myself."

"What?"

"When you called," I say, "I had an accident. I need to go to the hospital."

I hang up on him then, dial Chuck's number, ask him to come over. When he hears exactly how I cut myself, he starts to laugh. The sound does more to restore my sanity than anything he could've said. It isn't until the ride home, after the wait in the clinic for the physician's assistant to drive over from Colville, that I realize what has happened.

Walter has tried to get in touch with me. How appropriate that blood has been spilled. Too bad it happens to be mine.

※

Even with a bandaged hand, I manage to mount two-by-fours on the wall. They form a rectangle, sixteen by eight feet. Rene takes the day off from the kitchen, lets her next-door neighbor cook so she can hold the wood while I drive in the screws. We work along the back wall, where the tables have been cleared out to make way for us. The customers are intrigued, staring at us as if we are on display. They try to talk to me while they're eating tuna salad and fries, men the age of my grandfather and younger. They are used to looking at materials and visualizing the end result, but none of them can imagine what I'm putting together. It disturbs the men to see me so confident with tools, to watch Rene lifting heavy loads. They offer to help. We both decline. The truth is that we're having a good time.

I still haven't told Rene much about what I plan to do. I'm not exactly sure myself, although the pieces are coming together. For the most part, she trusts me, but even she has a doubt or two.

"Can I get one promise?" she asks as I stand on a milk crate to reach the right height.

"Sure."

"Nothing having to do with dead things."

I smile. "Depends how you define dead."

When I am ready, I will mix a small batch of white plaster, fine dust from a fifty-pound bag, enough water to create a paste. Once a section of plaster is spread along the wall, that will be the difficult stage. At that point, I will have to paint quickly enough to finish the work before the plaster completely dries, so the color can soak in before the plaster hardens. The technique was standard in the High Renaissance, but I cannot create walls of fresco like those artists did. I don't have a school of students, a legion of apprentices to draw and trace. I will settle for what I can manage by myself.

*

When I get home, there is a forest green luxury car in my driveway. I drive past it slowly, on my way down to the barn. There is no sign of the owner, either in the car or on the property. When I look up, I can see someone moving down by the horses. I take my hammer out of my toolbox.

When the figure finally emerges, I am struck dumb. I climb down from the truck, slam the solid door hard so it latches right. He looks at my boots, heavy and black with waffle soles and two pairs of wool socks underneath, and smiles.

It is hard to fathom, Walter standing in front of me, not wearing black, not as thin as he used to be. He has grown a goatee, which makes him look like a character from an old movie, Errol Flynn as Robin Hood.

"What are you doing here?"

"You say that like we live on different planets."

"I just never pictured you here. Not in a million years." It is ironic, I think, after all that time in New York when I would have gone out of my way to avoid him.

"I got worried," he answers, putting his hands in the pockets of his jacket. "That call last night, I couldn't figure it out."

I held up my left hand. "I was working on some frames and the phone rang. Glass broke."

"Is it bad?"

"Thirteen stitches."

He shakes his head. The bump on his nose gives his profile a bit of character, the extra layer of flesh seems to insulate him. His color is high, healthy. He was always handsome, but now he seems comfortable, as if he has settled into himself.

"I didn't know how long you'd be gone. I thought I'd better wait." There is a tentativeness in the way he speaks.

"So you've been waiting?"

He looks at his watch. I can see him calculating the time difference in his head. "Not long. An hour and a half."

"Jesus. You must have left New York at seven this morning."

"Six." He reaches into the inside pocket of his jacket, a nervous, face-saving gesture that he stops halfway. I don't smell cigarette smoke. I wonder whether he has quit.

"I have a check for you," he said. "From the gallery. Your percentage, plus a cash advance on materials for the next show. A new contract."

The talk of business comes as a relief. At least it is a place to start. "Still acting like Stieglitz?"

Walter doesn't answer that. Instead, he looks up at the rafters, the wide open space at the crown of the building. What he doesn't know is that I see angels there, corn-husk dolls clothed in horsehair and satin. I plan to fashion wings out of pine boughs, swathed in muslin. It may not bring the Virgin back, but it will show her I have not forgotten the layer of green just under the surface, the fresh smell of spring under the snow.

"No wonder you love it here," he says.

I walk into the workshop. Walter follows. I feel rather than see him duck his head to get through the low doorway. I expect a reaction like Chuck's, some surprise at how twisted I have become. I have taken a collection of train-flattened dimes and turned them into oval faces, marionette heads, with animal bones for the skeleton bodies. Copper wiring holds them together, finger and knee and shoulder joints. Walter does not flinch.

"It's freezing in here," he says instead. I flip on the space heater, which roars into red life. I run water into the coffeepot.

I watch as Walter turns, hands still in his pockets, staring up at the bottoms of dangling feet.

"I could pack these up and sell them tomorrow," he says, "the marionettes. Very portable. Very kitsch."

"My work isn't kitsch," I say.

"Jesus. Lighten up, Joanna. I thought you would've gotten over it by now."

"Gotten over what?" In my head, I dare him, I dare him to bring up the subject of the painting he'd destroyed, the face that was somehow mine and Chad's and his. I stare straight at him, but he doesn't look my way.

"The way we talk." By *we* he means art dealers. "I personally don't think there's anything close to kitsch here. But you know that's the way it'll get marketed eventually—they're small pieces, personal, dolls. That's the reality. All I'm saying is that we can include them in the deal if you want. Clear out some space here to do some more work."

"Space isn't really at a premium anymore."

Walter reaches out to touch one of the dolls. He twists a single braid of horsehair between his fingers. His back is to a wall where some drawings of Florence still hang. But he saw them on the way in, couldn't have missed the thick black lines. The dolls are just a diversion, the easiest thing in the room to think about.

"Is your hand really okay?" he asks, not looking at me.

"It'll be fine."

"I told them they should tell you. About me. About my part in the offer. I told them you'd find out."

My throat suddenly feels thick. I clear it once, twice, but can't shake the feeling that he is telling the truth, even though I don't want to believe him, don't want to be put in the position where I forgive him this thing, forgive him anything.

And at the same time I can hear everything we used to be in the tone of his voice—he holds the key to the Sistine Chapel in the palm of his hand. He is the reason I can afford to be here, holed up on property for which I can actually pay taxes. I remember all the ways I thought he felt like family.

"I would like to think I've changed some since we knew each other," he says, finally. "I'd like to think I've grown."

"You shouldn't have attacked Chad."

"You think I don't know that?"

"You shouldn't have attacked me," I say, and then I am the one who turns away, because I am determined not to let him see me cry. The tears fill my chest and my head, they stack up hot and dusty behind my eyes.

There is an electric buzz in the air from the heater. Now we are artificially, superficially, in this pocket of warm space. I want the smell of lilacs and the feel of cemetery grass under my cheek. What I get instead is the smell of Walter's cologne, a musk that doesn't belong anywhere in my world, and the feel of the rough workbench wood under my fingers.

"No," he says, from someplace far away. "But you shouldn't have been so afraid."

The regret I feel washes over me. Tears spill down my cheeks.

*

I sit with Walter on the hillside behind the house, in the clearing where Frank built a fire pit in a simple lean-to. I wouldn't have dragged him up here, not in the winter, not through the snow, except he wanted a rugged outdoor experience. That's what he called it, putting on the snowshoes, pulling a plastic kid's sled up the hill, a sled piled with wood and matches and a shovel to clear out the pit. His calves will be sore in the morning. I don't tell him that.

I arrange kindling over a mountain of paper while Walter puts slick green garbage bags over the cedar benches so we can sit. I watch the way the kindling catches, heat rippling against the cold air. I add a small stick, then two, then three. It will snow soon, I can tell by the clouds. They hang fat and low and full. The air smells wet. Walter holds his hands and feet out to the fire.

"I'm glad you've come back here," he says.

"And why is that?"

"Because it's obviously where you belong."

I don't know how to answer that. "You seem to be doing well," I finally say.

"You sound surprised."

"It's just that you seem so . . ."

"Well-adjusted?"

"I wouldn't have put it that way."

"Amazing what three years of therapy will do. It forces you to start telling the truth."

I would've been willing to hear the truth, I almost say, but then I hold back the words. I poke a stick into the fire, watching the sparks fly into the air.

"Do you know where the money came from?"

I don't have to ask which money, just shake my head.

"My mother sent it to me, wired it to a bank, as long as she didn't know what I was doing with it, as long as she didn't hear from me. She was so ashamed that I had turned out to be gay that she would've rather given me the entire fortune than admitted it."

"So what changed?"

"What makes you think anything has changed?"

"She obviously hired you."

"The gallery? She didn't do it out of some sense of loyalty. She did it because I turned out to be good at what I did." He leans forward, taking his hands out of his pockets, resting his elbows on his knees. "I took a couple of artists from the villa and started to represent them commercially. I used the blood money to open a small gallery. Your Czech friend?"

"Tomas?"

"He did an installation last year in Piazza San Marco in Venice as part of Carnevale. You can't believe the exposure he got. He sells now for a fair amount of money."

"I never thought his work was that good."

"It isn't. That's the point. But he pretends it's good. I pretend it's good. If you have the right kind of hype, who's going to admit they don't like his work?"

"So the emperor has no clothes."

Walter opens my thermos, pours hot cocoa into the cup, passes it over to me. "Except in your case. Your work is actually everything we said it was. That's why I went ahead with trying to secure you for Graham."

"It was your idea?"

"Packaged right, I knew the show would make money. I also knew my mother would give me more independence in the business."

I don't answer. If money had been his only motivation, a man like Walter could have created a dozen opportunities, just by trolling the East Village.

"Of course," he says reluctantly, as if he is not sure how I will take the news, "it's obviously because I think the work should be seen." Walter looks away from the fire, up into the woods. Then he looks back at me.

His words come out in a rush, as if he had made up his mind to say certain things if we ever met again. I don't ask him how he feels about my work, but he tells me anyway. As he speaks, the years seem to fall away, and we could be in Florence, standing on top of Brunelleschi's dome, holding hands and pretending that someday we would be giants, that the city itself would bow to us.

"You distill whole thoughts into single images," Walter says. "And those images are of things that you've seen that I will never see. I'll never see women the way you see them, or barns or sky or bones. Then you put it all down, and I feel it. Physically. The way I felt when I was eight and no one would speak to me at the dinner table. It's as if I'm sitting there and I have nothing. I have no one. And then I look at your painting and hear the words in what you paint, the stories of what has happened to you, and I feel close to another human being."

Snowflakes start to fall. First lightly, a meandering drift, then thicker, heavier, the beginnings of a blizzard. I lean back in my seat and watch the sky fall down on me.

"You're not making it back to Spokane tonight," I say. Even if he gets in his car right now, the roads will be blocked by the time he gets halfway to the airport.

"Is that all right?"

It is difficult to predict what will give and what will last. What looks sturdy from the outside can crumble under its own weight. What seems fragile may have a tensile strength that lends itself to bruises. Until he came to visit me, I would not have bet on my friendship with Walter. I would have been wrong.

I open my mouth, but not to answer Walter's question about staying over. I open my mouth wide to let the snowflakes in.

※

Luckily, I have more than enough groceries for one night of being homebound. I put water on for pasta, Walter drinks a cup of coffee. In the course of making small talk, I tell him that the reporter from Spokane has been calling me.

"Did you see the article in the *Times*?" Walter asks.

I pull a pan of bread out of the oven. It is toasted dark so I can soak it with olive oil, rub whole cloves of garlic over the surface. "Actually, I didn't."

"You are the only person on the face of the planet who wouldn't have read your own press."

I could tell him the story about Jerry Baker, but decide to save it for another time. Walter pulls a sheaf of paper out of his briefcase. "Here's the standard bio we did on you. It lists the information Graham gathered, plus some quotes that I remembered, some stuff that I thought would sound good and not offend you too deeply. You should look it over, then we can use it to send out to anybody who wants to talk with you."

"You make it sound as if there will be a flood."

"Maybe not at first. But they'll ask you fewer questions if you have the packet already prepared. They'll also be more likely to get it right. In this market, someone may actually come out to speak with you. Not in New York."

Outside, the snow is coming down thick. It isn't even five o'clock, but darkness has already settled in.

I have to ask him. "Have you spoken to Chad?"

"About six months ago. He's living in Washington."

"Of course he is."

"Did you see him on Jim Lehrer? They interviewed him about the crisis in the Balkans."

"I haven't had a television for a long time."

"Just as well. He's working on Capitol Hill. Legislative aide to Senator . . ." As I listen to his voice, I see a picture of it all, as clearly as if it is being drawn in front of me. I see Chad in a blue suit with a red tie, a leather briefcase, a short haircut, and a close shave. He walks up marble steps, striding down a hallway on the way to a hearing. His posture is straight, his grin is ready. He remembers everyone's name.

Walter clears his throat, mentions that Chad has a sketch of mine hanging over his mantel. His cello sits in the corner, where it remains unplayed.

"Let me guess: it's one of the drawings I did of him."

Walter laughs in a way that I know I am right. "It should be worth something someday."

"To be honest," I say, and Walter raises an eyebrow in mock fear, "I'm surprised he'd even talk to you."

"There's this place near his house, a bar that serves these gin and tonics. The gin comes in a full glass, and the tonic is just a bottle on the side. You drink straight iced gin to make room for the mixer." Walter makes a motion with two fingers to show how big the gin glass was. "This was in July, ninety degrees out, ninety percent humidity. Chad said it was the best drink he ever tasted."

"So you pretty much followed him into this bar and bought him a drink."

"Pretty much."

I can imagine that all too easily. "Some things don't change."

"No," Walter says simply. He gets two wineglasses out of the cupboard. "He hasn't settled down, in case you're wondering."

I was, but wouldn't have admitted it.

"And it's not as if we had a whole lot to talk about. Not anymore."

"Why did you go at all?"

He shrugs. "Same reason you're curious."

"And why exactly is that?"

"He's a measure of who we used to be."

I think of the day in the park when Walter and I sat together, envious, watching Chad concentrate, intent on his bocce throw. I have often thought of him in the colors of that afternoon, bright and shining, jewel-toned. I realize now that we handed him a kind of power he never should have had.

$$*$$

I draw the prototype for the main figure in the center of the fresco. I start very early in the morning, long before the sun comes up. Walter is sleeping on an air mattress in the front bedroom where Frank died. I wasn't exactly expecting visitors.

I have Rene's photographs around me, but I'm not ready to work with them yet. If my art, as Walter suggests, is made up of words, then I need to translate the mystery of imagination, the glory of worlds that exist only in my head. I want to find the language of miracles and write it in green, distinct enough for others to read. I go back to that night, just before Frank died, closing my eyes and feeling the vision pass across the surface of my skin. For the first time, I use a pen and paper to capture the image of the Madonna, not only what she looked like, but how she made me feel. I try to capture the spirit of prophecy that lit on me once and may never come again.

✳

Walter leaves the next afternoon with a hug and a kiss and Aaron's phone number in his pocket. It gives me a perverse kind of joy, thinking of the two of them, arguing together. There is a contract on my desk, one that I will sign in front of a notary public and send back to Graham.

Basking in the warmth of one reconciliation, I dial Jack's number. I would expect at the sound of his voice to feel nervous, but I don't. I can hear the television in the background, the artificial sound of an announcer and the shouts of the crowd. I don't say my name, don't ask him how he is.

"Why didn't you marry her?" I ask.

"Let me switch phones," Jack says. After some juggling, he picks back up. Whatever room he sits in is dead silent.

"Why didn't I marry her?"

"Yeah."

"You wouldn't happen to want to chat first—ease into the difficult stuff?"

He sounds confused, but I have little patience for him. Or maybe I have little patience for myself anymore. "It's important," I say.

"Of course it's important. It's just that you never even

met her, and now you expect me to summarize the whole relationship in one sentence over the phone?"

"More or less."

He laughs. "This is so typical of you. You don't bring it up for months. And now we have to talk about it right this second."

"Do you forgive me?" And in that question I am apologizing for all the pain that I caused him. I ask it in a quiet voice and wait for the answer.

Jack takes his time. I'm glad he doesn't blurt out some flip comment as if he doesn't know exactly what I am talking about. "I didn't. At first. And I'm not even talking about the other guy. I spent a long time just being angry at the fact that you moved so far away."

"You were one of the people who told me to go."

"I know that. But I was an idiot."

I shake my head. It isn't that simple. I can't conceive of a life without Florence, my work without exposure to Brunelleschi and the others. It would've meant no Lena, no saints, no children, no show. I would not trade those experiences for him, not even now. "I'm sorry about Chad," I say.

"I was angry about it for a long time. But then I realized you couldn't have known how I felt. I could've handled things better too."

"I left you."

"I think, when you get right down to it, we left each other."

I have to ask him. "Am I the reason you didn't marry her?"

"I'm going to be home in a week. We could take a walk or something."

"Please."

"I would really like to be able to see your face."

In my mind, I am thirteen. I climb over the edge of the railing, carefully. I stare down at the dark water. I will ask this once more and then never again.

"Was it because of me?"

I don't hear anything from his end of the phone, not even breathing. My fall is rapid, straight down and freezing, as if my life is over. I will kill Chuck, I will kill Walter, I will kill myself, anyone who put me up to this, this stupid confession, this attempt to recover what we never had.

"Of course it was because of you. After all this time, how could you not know that I love you?"

His words burn my throat, the insides of my lungs. The water, when I hit, is softer than I imagined.

✳

The Lincoln Continental slides through the snow to a stop in front of Rene's. This time I am actually wearing halfway respectable clothes, jeans and boots and a navy sweatshirt smeared with shades of white and gray. Rene has two cups of coffee waiting for the photographer and the reporter from Spokane when they come through the door. The woman is as ridiculous as I remember, wearing salt-and-pepper wool slacks and shiny black boots, as out of place in this diner as anyone could be. I wash my hands in Rene's industrial sink, while Ms. Barnes winds up into a short speech. She mentions the phrase "give and take." I want to stop to ask her what exactly she intends to give me, but then I reconsider. Rene is watching and will be appalled if I don't mind my manners. For her, this reporter is something special; for her the article could mean cold hard cash.

I sit across from Ms. Barnes in a booth, intrigued by the deep lines on either side of her mouth. When she tries to probe too deeply into the death of my mother, I discourage her with a shake of my head. I refer her back to Walter's sheet of biographical information. I see it in her eyes, that she is intimidated by me, worried I will cut the interview short, leaving her with nothing.

While she is asking me questions, writing down brief answers in a leather-bound book, Kip, the photographer, looks around obliquely, turning his head a little, using his eyes up and down and around, into corners, searching for clues. He is careful not to step on my materials on the floor, the photographs from my collection, from newspapers and magazines, the models for the landscapes and portraits I have already started.

I plan to include bits and pieces of the past in fictional combinations—a mayor, a horse, an Indian, a tourist, a bum who stumbled off the railroad tracks looking for work. In preliminary drawings, I lay farm equipment at their feet.

Hazel's pictures have provided close-ups for these, details of truck parts and circular saws. I set food on a table, cherry pie and a whole turkey, a dog for good measure, panting underneath. In the background sits the schoolhouse with tiny colored pieces of paper stuck up in the windows, finger-paint blue hands and cutout snowflakes. Inside stands a wizened teacher only I can see, a Depression-era woman in a faded print dress and heavy black shoes. She has perfectly rolled auburn hair.

Ms. Barnes looks down at her list of preprepared questions. "Where do you come up with your ideas?"

I stare at her for a moment. The question is not where I get my ideas, but where I do not. How can I ignore the weird scenes hidden in my memory, the bend of the river close to the railroad bridge, the school yard where I spent those silent months?

I shrug and smile. "It all just comes out."

She doesn't like that answer, I can tell. "Just comes out?"

"You act as if it's strange that I do this."

"I wouldn't say that."

"Look at drawings by children," I say, remembering Nia. "They'll make you eat your heart out. Color. Composition. You ask a kid to draw lonely and she'll put down a page of gray with purple at the edges. You ask a kid to draw peace and she'll draw clouds. That's better than what I do. We lose so much as we get older. If anything, that's what I think is strange."

The reporter doesn't write much. Instead, she retreats into another safety question.

"So where have you found your inspiration?"

"Here."

"No," she smiles a patronizing smile that means I haven't understood her, "I mean for your art."

She wants me to say Italy. She wants me to trot out the name of some famous painter. She persists in thinking that I am so different from her, that I see a separate world from the one we both live in.

I look across at Rene's counter and see Frank lifting fence posts out of the back of his truck. He puts on leather gloves before tackling the barbed wire. I see Jack having a cup of coffee, eating french fries with brown gravy on the side. Rene talks on the phone, and with the receiver in the curve of her neck, light coming in from the picture window, she looks like a Madonna, covering tuna salad with plastic wrap.

"I've learned just as much about art in this town as I have anywhere else." It doesn't matter to me whether this woman believes me or not. It just matters that I say it.

✳

Before they leave, Kip pulls me away to take some posed shots of me mixing plaster. Ms. Barnes goes in back to use the rest room. Without her there, the diner reverts back to its comfortable self, neither more nor less than what it actually is, a place where people gather, a place where people eat.

"My sister," the photographer says casually, "makes these houses out of cardboard. They're three-dimensional with different stories, furniture, the whole bit."

I blink against the flash, make a noncommittal noise to show I am listening. I am vain enough to wonder whether I am holding my mouth too straight, whether it is a line that will make me look stern.

"And she keeps passing them off as nothing."

"But they're not."

"Maybe you could talk to her."

"I don't get to Spokane much."

He frames a shot. "I could bring her out. She could really stand to see this."

I think about that for a moment, vaguely startled that he would consider me a role model. It occurs to me for the first time that this contract with Graham Easton means many things, not just money in the bank for taxes and repairs.

"If she really wants to see something, she should see my farm."

If this girl doesn't mind working with hair, I could set her to brushing the horses, tying up bundles into wigs for marionettes. She will make the acquaintance of my grandfather and learn what it is like to build a shrine.

"We'd have to do it after Christmas."

He nods, keeps shooting.

"You know," I say, "your Ms. Barnes is a real idiot."

"You're not the one who has to work with her."

The photograph that finally makes the paper is the one Kip takes at that precise moment. It is a good shot, well-framed—he catches me exactly at the moment I start to laugh.

※

Jack calls from Seattle, where he is forced to stay because bad weather has closed the mountain passes. Rene watches the weather reports all day on the tiny portable television she set on the counter. Snow keeps most customers away. It isn't quite dangerous yet, but it will be by the time it gets dark and the temperature drops back down below freezing. Rene talks to Jack with the phone held between her shoulder and her cheek—with her free hands she stirs soup and packs crackers and cans of vegetables into a box for me to take home.

I paint with a roller and listen to her half of the conversation. I am embarrassed by the way my stomach jumps, just knowing he is on the other end of the phone, the way my stomach falls, realizing he won't be able to visit the way he planned. I mask emotion by not turning to the phone at all, pretending to concentrate on the way the cream I have chosen for the back wall covers the sickly yellow.

When Rene holds out the phone, saying Jack wants to speak to me, I step squarely into the flat paint pan. Rene starts to laugh, tells Jack what I have done. Cream-colored latex seeps in between the waffle squares of my boot.

"Shit." I bend to get a piece of paper bag, place it under my paint-soaked boot, and I slide, one-footed like a hunchback, over to the linoleum counter. "Shut up," I mutter to Rene, but she laughs anyway. She knows I am only pretending to be calm, that there is every cause in the world for laughter.

The picture on the television has switched to a statewide weather map. It is a balmy fifteen degrees in Spokane, thirty degrees in Seattle. I imagine the roads in between, the people in houses and apartment buildings and mobile homes along the way, the acres of open, barren, frozen land.

"Hey," Jack says, "forgive me if I'm a few days late?"

Rene comes around, motions to me to sit down. She starts to unlace my boot. "Of course," I answer. Rene has small hands, narrow fingers with long nails that easily dig in under the laces to loosen them. She takes the boot, paint-soaked and age-molded to the exact shape of my foot, over to the door, puts it out in the snow.

"You don't sound too sure."

"I'm just a little disappointed." I have a hole in the toe of my wool sock. I curl the foot behind my other leg so Rene won't see it.

"If I didn't know better, I'd think you were looking forward to seeing me."

"Jack."

Rene breaks in. "I hate to cut you off, but it's coming down harder out there. We should both get home."

"Call me when you know," I say to him.

"You'll be the first."

I pause long enough to hear the weight of feeling on his end of the phone. "Love you," he says.

"I love you too."

I hang up the phone. On the counter are the sketches of my fresco cycle, an outline of what I will draw, quickly and without detail, on the plaster when it is in the beginning of that in-between stage, not too wet, not too dry. And then I will fill in the detail, working until I am finished. This kind of painting is both physically challenging and a mental drain. I had been wondering whether I wanted to start it so close to Jack's visit, whether I would be able to finish before I opened the door to let him in.

"Rene?"

"Yeah, hon'." She has a scarf wrapped around her face, a nylon parka with fur around the hood.

"I think I'm staying."

"Here? You'll get snowed in."

"I got everything here I've got at home." Right now, there is no one who will worry that I am late. No one will be waiting up for me to walk through the door. "Besides, worse comes to worst, Chuck'll dig me out by late afternoon."

"This is weird. Even for you."

"Thanks for all the faith you have in me."

"Seriously. If the power goes out."

"If the power goes out, I make a fire in your wood stove and turn on the propane lanterns. Same thing I'd have to do at home, because if it goes out here, it goes out there." That much is true. No matter where I am, I will be safe. No matter where I am, I will be warm. "Honestly. It's the only way I can finish before Jack gets here."

Rene shakes her head, wishes me good luck. She leaves the key on the counter so I can lock the door when I leave. Almost before she is gone, I have begun to erase her from my mind. I erase them all from my mind, until there is nothing in front of me except a slab of white and all the people I have yet to create.

I step outside briefly, to catch a breath of fresh air before I begin. Balanced on one leg, I wipe my boot in a bank of snow. In the dark, fat wet flakes fall on me. Across the street, a light illuminates the road, colors the snow as it comes in at an angle, driven by cold wind. The silence is alive; it blankets people I have known forever, a landscape I will always know.

Back inside, my cheeks red with cold, I turn on the tap, mixing water into the plaster. It will warm to the touch as it dries. I apply it thickly, pushing white paste into the corners of the frames with a trowel.

I do not think about Jack. I do not think about God. But they are both with me as I pick up the brush, roll it in color to hone the fine point. I start with Frank, the expression on his face years ago, at midnight, when I asked him where I fit in, when I asked him to lay out my life for me so I would not have to do it myself. I paint our house, our barn, our woods, the bridge, the fences. Hazel is there, on horseback, out in the field where she took so many pictures, set apart because that is where she chose to be.

The Virgin Mary will stand above it all, dressed in a robe made of peacock feathers, a gentle smile on her face. Her skin will be dark, the color of the Indians, the color of the Mexicans who come in the summer to pick fruit. She will have Father Sandoval's straight black hair. And at her feet, the rest of us will cluster, buildings and animals and people, under the protection of her arms. Our crops will grow green, the apples and alfalfa fat and ripe. The light streaming from her fingers will heal the hard-hearted, and teach us all we know of love. We will swim in it, the light from her fingers, drown in it and die with smiles on our faces.

Acknowledgments

My thanks to:

Joe, Patricia, and Kathe, the real artists.

Marsha and Simon, for their feedback on early drafts.

The Miller and Rhodes families, for use of their cabins.

Paul and Brad, for pointing me in the right directions.

Ethan and Luke, who have shown more enthusiasm for this project than I had a right to expect.

And finally my family and Monte—your love has been a blessing to me.